SHORT *Stories* II

MYSTERIES
THRILLERS
HISTORICAL

RICH DiSILVIO

Cover art & photo of Lion, interior illustrations, photos of FDR and Churchill busts and the paintings of *The Divine Crucifixion* and *Tchaikovsky Memorial* by © Rich DiSilvio. Photos of historical figures and artwork of famous artists are in the public domain, courtesy of Wikipedia.

Author's Website: www.richdisilvio.com

- - - - - - - - - - - - - - - - - -

Names: DiSilvio, Rich
Title: Short Stories II: Mysteries, Thrillers, Historical / Rich DiSilvio
Description: New York, USA: DV Books, an imprint of Digital Vista, inc.
Identifiers: ISBN 978-0-9983375-6-2 (paperback) |
ISBN 978-0-9983375-7-9 (eBook)
Subjects: Short Stories | Mysteries, Thrillers | Artists, Composers | WWII | Short stories, American--History and criticism
Illustrations/Photos: 14

Contents

SHORT Stories II

II

MYSTERIES
THRILLERS
HISTORICAL

RICH DiSILVIO

THE PHANTOM FORGER

Bernard Higley gasped as a large flake of paint peeled off of Antonello da Messina's long-lost masterpiece, the *Messina Madonna*. He had merely wiped the canvas with a fine linen cloth to remove what appeared to be a smudge, but a small chunk of oil paint peeled away and fell to the floor. He moved closer, in shock, as his eyes widened.

Bernard had been enthralled to acquire the prized find, being that it was last recorded as being seen in 1608. As curator of the Cloisters museum in upper Manhattan, Bernard Higley was making preparations for a huge promotional campaign to herald the historic find, along with presenting three other recent acquisitions dating from the Renaissance era. But the *Messina Madonna* was the focal point, and Bernard had intentions of premièring the work early next year, in February of 1979, the five-hundredth anniversary of Messina's death.

As Bernard stepped even closer, he could feel his heart erratically accelerating as beads of sweat formed along his receding hairline. "Dear Lord! This can't be!" he frantically whimpered. He turned and ran past the stacks of paintings and priceless artifacts in the museum's storage chamber to the phone, and placed a call to the only person he could entrust to help him, Armand Arnolfini.

Thirty minutes later, at 6:52 AM, Armand entered the medieval complex. The Cloisters museum was an historic assemblage of five ancient French cloisters that had been dismantled and shipped to New York in the 1930s to be reconstructed, along with their exquisite gardens. The munificent gift was by John D. Rockefeller Jr., who had also purchased the scenic property across the Hudson River to ensure it stayed undeveloped, as not to destroy the Cloisters' bucolic ambience. Armand walked past a series of Gothic archways, ancient tapestries and wood-carved bas-reliefs, then descended to the lowest level.

Bernard ran to greet him, as he gushed, "Armand! I'm so happy you could make it, especially at this early hour and on such short notice. I do apologize, but this is a most urgent and distressing matter."

"I sensed that on the phone, Bernie," Armand said as he yawned and massaged his sleepy eyes.

Armand Arnolfini was six-foot-two with jet-black wavy hair, finely chiseled features, and a muscular body from his three years of playing professional fútbol when he lived in Italy eight years ago. "What's the problem?"

Bernard swallowed hard. "I recently purchased a Messina, the *Messina Madonna*. And—"

"*The* 'Messina Madonna!?'" Armand blurted, surprised, and now awake.

Armand was not a typical private detective, as he previously worked for the FBI heading their Art Crimes division, which unfortunately disbanded due to America's lack of interest in the field. And that his father had been the curator of the Uffizi Gallery for twenty-two years and a professor of art history for many years thereafter, Armand was an expert in his own right, so he knew well the history and significance of Messina's long-lost portrait.

Antonello da Messina might not have risen to the high echelon of fame as da Vinci or Michelangelo, but it was Messina, who, being twenty-two years older than Leonardo, introduced the art of oil painting in Italy, having learned the technique from the alleged inventor himself; the Flemish master Jan van Eyck. As such, Messina had played a pivotal role in enlightening and inspiring the budding crop of painters in Italy who would propel the Italian Renaissance to the apex of creativity.

Meanwhile, Bernard hesitated in his response, "Well, uh, yes, it's the one and only *Messina Madonna*, Armand. However—"

"That's fantastic, Bernie! You must be overjoyed to acqu—"

"Hold on!" Bernard interjected. "I must tell you what happened."

As Armand's elation turned quizzical, Bernard continued, "I was simply wiping a smudge off the canvas when a chunk of paint peeled off."

Armand's concern transformed into a smile. "You had me worried, Bernie. We both know plenty of restorers who can repair it."

Bernard grimaced. "Armand, yes, it can be repaired, but that would only hide its dishonorable sins. What has been revealed through the portal that chip presented is most disturbing."

Armand squinted. "Are you saying there's another painting underneath?"

"Yes, but it's not an earlier painting, Armand. That would have been a relief, as it could explain it being a previous work by Messina that the master decided was substandard, and thus painted over it."

Armand rubbed his chin. "So you're saying there is a newer work underneath. How can that be? Are you sure?"

"Come, see for yourself."

Bernard escorted Armand to the Cloisters' subterranean conservation and storage chamber, with its modern nineteen-seventies tiled floor, muted-white walls, and where the air temperature and humidity was precisely controlled. Walking past a string of artifacts and tapestries from the medieval to Renaissance eras, they arrived at the *Messina Madonna,* which was sitting on a large oak easel.

Armand's eyes widened as he took a double-step to inspect it closer. "Good God!" His head swung toward Bernard. "A newer work, indeed!" He turned back to the painting and its disturbing aperture that Bernard had enlarged, thus revealing a large fragment of the unwelcome image underneath. "It appears to be a portion of a crucifixion. And, yes, by a modern surrealist."

"Exactly, Armand. Not being well versed in modern art, I am at a loss as to whom this mysterious artist might be. But more importantly, whom this repugnant forger of Renaissance masters must be, who didn't even have the decency to use a blank canvas. It's just an added slap in the face."

Armand leaned forward and peered behind the painting. He scratched the back of the canvas and smelled it, then looked back at Bernard. "It even looks and smells old."

"Yes, the forger somehow did a fine job of making the canvas appear old all right. Enough to fool my staff and I."

Armand gazed back at the aperture, and at the bright-colored paint beneath the dark-varnished veneer of the faux Renaissance oils. Pensively, he paused for a moment, then said, "I wonder if it's possible that the painting underneath is a masterwork by Magritte or Dali. The style fits."

Bernard shook his throbbing head. "Why on earth would someone cover a new masterwork with a fake old one?"

"One never knows what is and isn't possible, Bernie. My father had told me that during World War Two some museum officials had several of their masterpieces painted over with works by unknown artists to prevent Nazi thieves from stealing their priceless assets."

"Then I could only hope that what lies beneath this Messina is a Magritte or Dali, Armand. Only then could I recoup my financial blunder. I spent two hundred and fifty thousand dollars for this piece."

Armand cringed. "Ouch!"

"Ouch, indeed," Bernard uttered dejectedly. "We anticipated a Messina revival. But now those hopes are dashed. However, Jim Matteson, my restorer, is on his way here now to strip it completely. Then we shall have a better idea of what we're dealing with."

Three hours later, Jim had stripped the canvas of the faux Messina, revealing a startling vision of a crucifixion. The surreal vision was unlike anything Bernard or Armand had ever seen.

Armand stepped closer to inspect the unknown artist's brushstrokes and technique. "At first glance, Bernie, I thought it might be a Dali, since the famous old Spaniard painted a series of religious works back in the fifties. But the technique is different."

Bernard grimaced. "Well, you would certainly know better than I, Armand. Modern art is not my area of expertise."

"Nor is it mine, Bernie, as most of my experience and training had come from my father when I lived in Florence and visited him at the Uffizi. But I have always been drawn to the surrealists and have examined many works over the years, so I can say quite confidently that this crucifixion is not by Dali. But since Dali is still alive, perhaps we could ask him if he knows who this surrealist artist might be."

"I must say," Bernard said as his eyes scanned the canvas, "despite not being acquainted with surrealism, this rendition is quite stunning."

Armand gazed back at the tall, elongated canvas, which stood four-feet tall and two-feet wide. "It is rather dramatic, and akin to Dali's great masterwork of the same subject, even if Dali's technical prowess is superior." Armand studied the work for several moments, then added, "However, this composition conveys some very profound spiritual concepts that other crucifixions don't."

As they both stared at the mysterious work, they realized that the painting at first shocked the viewer with an unnatural sense of melodrama, yet the fantastical vision was clearly not intended to be a realistic portrayal of Jesus at Golgotha. Rather it was deeply symbolic with religious import.

The gargantuan cross, which towers over two other crucifixions of condemned souls, stood in a fog-laden valley, as the dark, cloudy sky parted to shed light on Jesus. Moreover, Jesus' colossal cross stood perfectly straight and true—unlike those of the two mortals beside him—and towered majestically above mankind, symbolically residing in the heavens, while mankind resided in the lower earthly realm, with craggy rocks and rough terrain; symbolic of the travails that mankind must endure in a precarious world.

Moreover, the convict that Jesus had absolved of sin was placed at his front, in partial light, while the other eternally damned soul resided at Jesus' back, in the shadows. What remained quite clear, however, was that the intense focal point of the divine drama was unquestionably Jesus. Hence, amid the dark and turbulent veil of clouds, which fittingly bemoaned the fateful event, God the Father's divine light miraculously parted the heavens to warmly embrace His son.

"A stunning work, indeed," Bernard said. "It's a Divine Crucifixion in every sense. But not knowing who this mysterious artist is, or was, leaves me in a most precarious position, Armand."

Armand turned and surveyed the room. "You said you purchased three other works recently. Were they from the same seller?"

"Yes, I bought them from Michel Tucci. He is an Italian fellow, fairly well known in the industry. How could he not be, he's ninety years old."

"Ninety!?" Armand nearly choked. "He's almost as old as Messina."

Bernard chuckled, then smirked. "Yes, Michel has been around for almost a century, but in retrospect, he hasn't sold that many paintings. And all of those transactions were in Europe. Nevertheless, he established a good reputation, so we felt confident in our purchase, especially since all the exposed rears of the canvases were tested as being authentic in age. Quite distressing, however, is that I tried calling Mr. Tucci, but his landlord answered. He said Michel had unexpectedly moved, without saying a word or leaving a forwarding address. He's vanished."

Armand squinted. "Hmm, I never heard of this Michel Tucci. But my father knows many contacts throughout Europe, so I'm confident he or someone he knows must have crossed paths with Signore Tucci."

"My thoughts, exactly, Armand."

"But first, we should inspect those three other acquisitions of yours, as I suspect they might be forgeries, as well."

Barnard recoiled with a shiver. "Good grief! I certainly hope not. A quarter of a million dollars lost thus far is more than enough for my weak heart to endure."

"Well, it's best if you face the grim reality now, Bernie, so we can make plans as to how to solve this mysterious crime."

Bernard instructed his technician to X-ray the three remaining pieces, being that the machine had been broken for two months and was recently repaired. Bernard and Armand both held their breath as the machine snapped the three films and the technician developed the X-rays. To Bernard's poor-old-heart's despair, all three indicated that surreal images existed underneath. Bernard then instructed Jim to strip the canvases by removing the top veneer of paint. However, as Jim stripped the last painting, Bernard and Armand shrieked, "Eureka!" and "Bingo!" respectively, when it revealed a very special clue. It was signed!

Armand smiled. "Well, Bernie, at least now we know the name of our mysterious modern artist."

Bernard shrugged. "Yes, but who the hell is Paolo Santanello?"

"Don't know. Never heard of him. I'll have to make some inquires. But it still doesn't explain who the nefarious forger is." Armand shook his head, baffled. "And why did the forger use Santanello's works of art to paint his fakes?"

Armand crossed his muscular arms as he pondered the enigma further. "Perhaps he's a rival or an enemy of Paolo's. Or possibly he simply purchased these unknown paintings and decided to use them for his criminal charade." He shook his head. "None of this makes much sense."

Bernard paused in thought, then said, "I just wonder if Michel Tucci knew if these were fakes, or if he was hoodwinked by the forger, as well?"

"Yes, there are several possible explanations, Bernie, but there's only one way to find out. It's time for me to seriously start my investigation."

Bernard sighed with a modicum of relief, knowing well Armand Arnolfini's impressive record for success. "So, what will be your first course of action?"

"I plan on catching a flight to Florence, Italy, to visit my dad. I sense this Michel Tucci fellow returned home and, as mentioned, my father has many connections in Italy and throughout Europe. What's more, the timing is right, as I'm overdue to see my Pa anyhow. Like Signore Tucci, he, too, is an old man. So, two birds, one stone, as they say."

Before catching his flight, Armand thumbed through his Rolodex and managed to contact Salvador Dali. He hoped the old master might know who Paolo Santanello might be, perhaps being a minor surrealist from the early years of the genre's birth. But the great Dali had no recollection of an artist by that name.

Armand then caught his flight on Alitalia and landed in Florence. He hopped on a rented Vespa and traveled over the Ponte Vecchio, past the Pitti Palace, and turned down the excruciatingly narrow Via Toscanella, where he arrived at his father's midsized but exquisite apartment. His father, Sergio, took almost two minutes to answer the door, but when he did, father and son embraced, warmly, lovingly.

"So good to see you, my son," Sergio said with a gracious smile that stretched across his wrinkled yet still handsome face. "What brings you home to Florence, work or pleasure?"

Armand smiled, with a touch of regret. "Well, both, Papa. But to be honest, work has lured me back, this time to a mysterious art crime, a forgery. Rather, four forgeries: one of the Renaissance master Messina, and three lesser-known artists from the same era, including Domenico Alfani, Antonio Boselli and Domenico Panetti."

Sergio's eighty-year-old eyes ignited with a sparkle, one not seen in many years. "Ah! How I miss being engaged in the passionate world of art, even if dealing with forgeries." He scratched his well-groomed head of gray hair with his wrinkled hand, which was adorned with a stunning Cellini-like golden ring, then slipped on his immaculately tailored, designer dinner jacket. "But I wonder why this forger chooses relatively obscure Renaissance artists. Surely they don't fetch anywhere near the price of a Raphael or a Titian, and the painstaking work that goes into these works is extremely intricate and time-consuming."

Armand walked over to the refrigerator and pulled out a Peroni. He extended it to his dad, who refused, and he popped off the top. He took a swig and savored the smooth barley malt flavor as it titillated his palate. With a swish of his tongue and a pucker of his lips, he swallowed, then said, "Good question, Pa. But I'm more interested in finding out who this forger is, because there's an additional mystery to this case; namely, all his forgeries are painted over the works of the same surrealist artist, a guy named Paolo Santanello. Have you ever heard of him? Or an art dealer named Michel Tucci?"

Sergio squinted as his mind took several attempts to start up, like an old gas-powered generator being started with a pull-string. After a few blinks his eyes began to glow. "Yes, yes! I vaguely recall a Signore Tucci. He was a small-time dealer of lesser-known artists, like the ones you mentioned, but nothing in particular or nefarious stands out about him. And this Santanello fella doesn't ring a bell, Armand. I'm sorry." He paused and rubbed his temple as a distant memory began to materialize in the dark and dusty abyss of his antiquated mind. He gazed at the wall, then up at the ceiling. His eyes oscillated, looking everywhere, yet nowhere in particular.

Armand put his bottle of beer down. "What is it, Pop?"

Sergio's wandering eyes suddenly stopped, then gazed at his son. "Ah! Yes, of course. I do recall a strange occurrence, it happened many years ago. I believe it was nineteen fifty-four, or was it five? Hmm, no, I think it was—"

"Never mind the date, Pop, what was it you remember?"

Sergio was bumped out of his data-seeking rut like a needle skipping on an LP, and he got back on track. He blinked hard and nodded with a smile of gratification, happy to have remembered something from his distant past. The biggest bane of his life was the slow and humiliating loss of his precious knowledge and memories. He grasped the lapel of his stylish jacket and boldly declared, "Clara, Clara Vandermeer."

Armand's lips twisted with an awkward smile. "Yes, that's just splendid, Pa. That's a very nice name. But what about Clara Vandermeer?"

Sergio teasingly paused, then with a proud smile, said, "Clara happens to be the curator of the Groeninge museum in Bruges, Belgium. It houses a fine selection of Northern Renaissance masters and several surreal works, including one by René Magritte." As Armand's eyes widened, Sergio added, "However, Clara had experienced some sort of incident when she started her surrealist collection, but I can't for the life of me recall what it was. Nevertheless, with her keen knowledge of Renaissance and modern surrealist works, I imagine she could be very helpful in your quest."

"Indeed she can!" Armand said with a warm grin. "I knew I could count on you, Papa. *Grazie!*"

"*Prego,*" Sergio replied. Yet his prideful face soon withered. "Does that mean you're leaving me already?"

Armand grasped his bottle of Peroni and took a short sip, his smile morphing into a solemn portrait of regret. "Well, I'll spend two days here with you, Pa, but unfortunately work beckons me, as it did you for so many years. I'm sure you can understand the magnetism of doing something you love."

Sergio glanced at his prized collection of high-quality giclee reproductions, featuring several masterpieces from the Renaissance and Baroque eras, then back at his ambitious son. "Very true, my boy, very true. Who am I to clip your wings when I soared with the greatest names in Renaissance art for so many years at the Uffizi Gallery, and had the good fortune of teaching that wealth of knowledge and culture to several younger generations?"

Armand lovingly wrapped his arm around his father and walked him up the spiral staircase to the top floor of the apartment. There they gazed out of a large picture window, as their line of sight traveled across the Arno River to see the splendid vista of the city of Florence, the cultural epicenter of the Renaissance with the majestic Il Duomo, along with the Uffizi Gallery and art academy where Sergio took much pride in Florence's rich past, a lifetime spent preserving a critical milestone of Western civilization.

Moments later they strolled down to the kitchen, where, together, they cooked a savory meal of hot antipasto, raviolis, and eggplant rollatini. They reminisced about their early days, when Armand lived in Florence, from his birth to the time he played for AC Milan, as well as sharing loving memories of Armand's dear mother, who had died of polio when Armand was only thirteen. Afterwards, they capped the night off with cappuccino and homemade tiramisu, Armand's favorite dessert, and bid each other good night.

Two days later, Armand arrived at the Groeninge museum in Bruges.

Clara approached him, wearing a stylish full-length dress and her gray hair pulled back in a bun. Her physique and skin didn't betray the fact that she was seventy-eight years old, as she said, "Welcome, Signore Arnolfini. Your father apprised me of your desire to speak with me, yet did not mention the topic of your interest. How can I help you?"

Armand's eyes, however, were drawn to the painting behind her, as he cordially shook her hand and said, "Excuse me, Mrs. Vandermeer, but I must see your *Portrait of Margareta van Eyck*."

Clara smiled; being used to men being drawn away by Jan van Eyck's masterful works. She had long ago resigned herself to taking second fiddle, as she graciously turned and pointed to the larger painting beside the famous portrait. "And that's van Eyck's second largest surviving panel, after his illustrious Ghent Altarpiece. It is the *Virgin and Child with Saints Donatian and George and—*"

"They're both magnificent!" Armand interjected, as he stepped closer, his eyes devouring them as if the tiramisu he had eaten two nights before. "I've always had an affinity for Jan van Eyck's work. Perhaps it's because my great, great ancestor was immortalized in his most famous painting."

Clara's head recoiled. "You're not saying you're related to Giovanni Arnolfini, are you? Certainly you jest."

"Why do you say that?"

Clara looked at Armand with reproachful eyes. "Because I had asked your father about that many years ago, and he said you were not related."

Armand chuckled. "Yes, my father can be very critical, as I'm sure you're well aware. It's his highly perceptive yet merciless eye as an art critic that had jaded him to van Eyck's masterpiece."

Clara squinted. "What's not to like?"

"Well, he whole-heartedly admires van Eyck's technical prowess, being perhaps the greatest technician in the Renaissance. Moreover, Jan's attention to detail and his precision of painting inert objects was second to none. However, my father abhorred many of van Eyck's figures, and of Giovanni in particular. He said our great ancestor did *not* look like a rigid corpse, or an ugly porcelain doll, and took it as a personal affront to our great Arnolfini name."

Clara's lips parted with a reflective smile. "That does sound like you father. Sergio was always a most brilliant and knowledgeable man, but aesthetics dominated his every-waking decision."

Armand nodded. "Yes, but while I can be just as critical, I can also overlook such human flaws to recognize a masterpiece in overall execution. The composition and technique of the *Arnolfini Portrait* is absolutely stunning, especially considering it was painted in fourteen thirty-four, some eighteen years before da Vinci was even born."

"You are absolutely correct, Signore Arnolfini. But I'm sure you did not come all the way to Belgium just to tell me of your famous relation to a Flemish masterpiece."

Armand chuckled. "No, not at all. I've come on business. I'm investigating a case for Bernard Higley at the Cloisters museum." As Clara nodded, acknowledging her acquaintance with the American curator, Armand continued, "He recently acquired four works by Italian Renaissance artists. However, all four were forgeries. But most peculiar still was that all four were painted over the works of a modern surrealist artist."

Clara gasped. "How awful! Poor Bernard."

Armand scanned the gallery as he inquired, "My father said you have an eye for old Renaissance masters and modern surrealists. Have you ever purchased works from a man by the name of Michel Tucci?"

Clara's eyes at first squinted, then opened wide. "Yes! In fact I did. I believe it was back in nineteen fifty-five."

Clara went on to explain how Michel Tucci had originally approached her attempting to sell the works of an unknown surrealist artist. Despite her interest in surrealism—even purchasing a Magritte, among others—Clara had refused Michel's offer, being that she wasn't in the market for unknown artists. However, a year later, Tucci returned, this time offering a splendid array of Flemish, German, Italian, and French artists from the Renaissance to Rococo eras. And despite those artists being lesser known, they were not *unknown*, and well worth the reasonable investment.

Armand's jaw twisted as his mind reeled. "Would you mind if I take a look at those acquisitions?"

"Of course not. Come, right this way."

As they entered another gallery, Clara pointed to six paintings. "Here they are." Her face was now marred with concern. "You're not suggesting that Michel sold me fakes, as well, are you?"

"It's a distinct possibility, Mrs. Vandermeer. I think it would be wise to have them X-rayed to see if they're forgeries."

Clara grimaced. "The mere thought of this makes me ill, Signore Arnolfini. We no longer have an X-ray machine, but I'll have an infrared reflectogram done. It's also noninvasive and will determine what exactly lies underneath the top layer of paint. And I'm hoping it's nothing more than base pigment."

An hour later, Armand and Clara found themselves in a back room, waiting impatiently as the technician scanned the works. The first one proved to be an original, but as the remaining five were scanned, they each revealed a painting underneath. Clara and Armand gasped, especially since all five appeared to be in the same style as the mysterious, surrealist artist Paolo Santanello.

Clara's face turned crimson red as she spat, "Where is this Michel Tucci!?"

Armand gazed solemnly at the paintings, then back at Clara. "I have no idea. I was hoping you might have some insights as to where he might be. I know he lived somewhere in Italy, but his last known whereabouts was in the United States, when he sold Bernard Higley those forgeries. Yet, when Bernard tried to contact him, his landlord said he had moved, with no forwarding address."

Clara glanced at the five fakes and grunted. "You can have them, they're worthless!"

Armand twitched. "I'm truly sorry for revealing this scam, Mrs. Vandermeer. I can only imagine how upset you must be. However, while I appreciate your offer, I couldn't possibly take them."

Clara shook her head and slammed the table. "Upset doesn't begin to explain how humiliated and deceived I feel!

Michel Tucci seemed like a nice respectable man, and I knew of several other curators who had purchased works from him, as well." She paused, then added, "Yet, I have not heard a word about him for many years, until this recent scam you've just mentioned at the Cloisters. Do you have any idea if Tucci knows these works are fakes, or is he being duped like us?"

"That's a good question, Mrs. Vandermeer, one that we've been asking, as well. But I aim to find out."

No sooner did he finish that sentence, than Clara's secretary entered the room. "Mrs. Vandermeer, there is an urgent phone call for you from a Mister Sergio Arnolfini. He wishes to speak to his son." Peering over Clara's shoulder, she added, "Is that him?"

Armand stepped briskly into view, fearing his father might be ill. "Yes, I'm his son. Where is the phone?"

Armand dashed to the main office and picked up the receiver. "Pop, what's wrong? Are you okay?"

Sergio's voice surged through the earpiece, "I'm fine, Armand. However, my dear friend, Anton Platzer, just called me. He's the curator at the Schwarzenberg Palace, in Prague. And get this, he just discovered that two recent acquisitions were revealed as forgeries!"

An electric chill ran down Armand's back. "Don't tell me, Michel Tucci was the dealer and Anton found surreal paintings underneath?"

"Exactly, Armand. Evidently, Tucci's fakes have spread like a virus."

Armand wrapped up his conversation with his father, then bid Clara farewell. Taking another flight, Armand landed in Czechoslovakia, and dashed to the Schwarzenberg Palace.

Anton Platzer greeted Armand with open arms and a broken heart. He explained how he had purchased the works of two minor artists: Hans von Aachen, a German painter of Northern Mannerism, and Norbert Grund, a painter of the Rococo style from Prague.

Armand examined the works, marveling over the skill and detail of the disparate styles of the forgeries, yet remained baffled about the forger's reason for painting over another artist's work. *Who would do such a thing, and why?* He thought.

"Mr. Platzer, my father informed me that you purchased these paintings from Michel Tucci, is that correct?"

"Yes. I can't believe that feeble old man sold me fakes," Anton huffed. "He seemed so sincere and kind. Not to mention that his sterling reputation had preceded him."

Armand glanced at the two paintings. "Do you have any idea where Tucci might be?"

"All I know is that he moved to the United States. I believe he is somewhere in New York."

"Are you sure he didn't move back home to Italy? He recently made a score in New York at the Cloisters museum and abandoned his apartment."

Anton shook his head. "No, I believe his trail here in Europe is too well worn and beginning to fall apart for him to remain here. It appears he is now staking out new territory." He scratched his head. "But does Tucci know that he's selling fakes, or is he just a blind fool, like all of us?"

"My guess is that he knows very well what he's doing. That all of his forgeries are painted over the same artist's works seems to indicate he or his forger knew this artist and didn't care much for his modernist bent. So either he or someone he knows covered them over with very skillful renditions of old masters, and he's making a pretty penny in the process."

"A pretty *penny*! Huh! That scoundrel fleeced me of fifty thousand dollars. And I hear Clara and Bernard, among others, have all lost more than that. I'll gladly contribute five thousand dollars to your investigation if you catch this despicable old weasel."

"Thank you, I aim to try, Mr. Platzer. I'll be in touch." Armand shook his hand and took his leave.

Catching a flight to JFK airport, Armand returned to his apartment on the Upper East Side, several blocks from the Metropolitan Museum of Art and the Guggenheim. As he sat on the couch watching an episode of *The Rockford Files*, his mind wandered. *If Michel Tucci came to America*, he thought, *he didn't come empty handed!*

He zapped the TV off with the remote, then called Peter Hansen, an old friend in the FBI. He asked Peter to scan all the manifests of air and sea freight shipments from Italy containing the name Michel Tucci. Peter obliged, and three hours later, Armand's phone rang.

"Hello? Peter?"

"Yeah, Arnolfini. It's Saint Peter. I came through for you. Your pal Michel had a large shipment made from Italy last year. Manifest number 83290. It was then delivered to an address in upstate New York on February third." Peter paused, then added, "I actually bought some property up in Wurtsboro. It's beautiful and peaceful, Arnolfini. You know, getting away from the rat race and all. Kind of like Green Acres." Peter then began singing the jingle, "Greeeen Acres is the place to be. Faaaarm livin' is the life for—"

"For Pete's sake, Pete! Stop clowning around! What's the address?"

Peter chuckled. "Okay, hold your piglets, Arnol...Ziffel."

"Don't be a ham, Pete! Because if you were, you'd have botulism."

Peter laughed, then snorted as he said, "Okay, okay, it was delivered to 157 Highview Terrace in Bloomingburg, New York. Do you need the zip code, too, Arnolfini?"

"No, that will do. I owe you one, Pete!"

"One?" Peter said. "How about a hundred and one!"

"Well, if you really want to start counting, I guess you'd have to sell your house in Brookville to pay *me* back."

Peter chuckled. "Very true, Arnolfini. You know I'm toying with ya. But you really should come up and see my property in Green Acres. There's a guy up there who, I swear, looks just like Mr. Haney. In fact, I think it *is* Mr, Haney!"

Armand finally laughed. "You're a knucklehead, Pete. But, okay, we'll have to hook up for dinner one day and checkout your property. But I have to run. This lead is a good one. Thanks again!"

Armand hopped in his brand new '79 gold Oldsmobile Toronado, which was released three months prior to the New Year, and turned on the radio. It was playing *Runnin' with the Devil* by a new band called Van Halen. Armand smirked as he thought how Michel Tucci was also running with the Devil. He then tuned in WQXR. He smiled; it was playing Franz Liszt's revolutionary *Second Piano Concerto*, a twenty-two-minute masterpiece of pure genius. He slammed the car into gear and headed upstate on the New York Thruway.

He crossed over the Tappan Zee Bridge, past the Ramapo rest stop, and headed west at Exit 16. Before long he came to Exit 114, then drove up the winding street, onto Highview Terrace, which eventually reached the peak of the mountain. As he gazed out, he was overcome by the lush panorama of the Hudson Valley, which spread out as far as the eye could see in all directions, with distant mountains sculpting the horizon.

What a spot! He thought. *A spot anyone would relish, especially an art dealer.* He chuckled. *Or even Mr. Haney.*

As he drove farther along the dirt country road, he came upon a startling sight, a towering A-frame chalet that stood majestically on the summit.

Armand scanned the area; there wasn't another house or person in sight. He turned off the engine and stepped out. The silence, seclusion, and sky-scraping perch atop the highest peak in the valley struck him at once as quite eerie, yet sublimely ethereal. Now he understood why people called areas like this God's Country. The Shawangunk Mountain Range had a special charm all its own.

As the thick cumulus clouds in the distance parted, a beam of sunlight shed its golden rays upon the valley and onto the tiny telephone poles below, which suddenly appeared like small crucifixes. The image of Santanello's surreal crucifixion came streaming back into his consciousness. Armand shook his head free of the mirage and walked up to the modern chalet. Gazing up at the peculiar, stylish structure, Armand was moved by the pyramidal shape that was so prominent in houses of worship or the grand pyramids of Egypt. He was expecting to find an unassuming hideout, certainly nothing like *this*.

He walked up the broad redwood deck and up to the large glass sliding doors. He rang the bell and waited.

No response.

He shifted from side to side, to see if he could peer through the curtains, but to no avail. He knocked on the glass door, but that too yielded no reaction.

Disheartened, Armand returned to his Toronado and drove down the mountain, making his way to the Shawanga Lodge. He rented a room and had a meal in the motel's restaurant, which fell drastically short of pleasing his cultivated palate. With his appetite at least satiated, he watched an episode of *Barney Miller*, then retired for the night.

Early the next morning, Armand drove back up to the A-frame chalet. As he approached the peak of the mountain, he slowed down. Parked on the gravel driveway was a yellow, Supercharged 1937 Cord 812 Coupe. He pulled up alongside the rare and precious automobile, with its distinctive flex-chrome exhaust pipes, and came to a stop. He gazed at the quarter-million-dollar car and shook his head, irritated: *And they say crime doesn't pay. Ha!*

He slid out of his Oldsmobile and climbed quietly up the deck and reached the sliding doors. Once again, he couldn't see past the sheer curtains to decipher Michel Tucci or any moving silhouette. He rang the bell.

Nothing.

He knocked on the glass doors.

Again, nothing.

Armand sighed as he dejectedly gazed at the ground, his mind reeling: *Where did the old swindler go? Or is the decrepit old crook just deaf?* He turned right and looked at the radiant '37 Cord. *The old geezer certainly has good taste though.*

On instinct, Armand turned left, where the glare from a patch of white birch trees reflected into his eyes. As he squinted, he noticed the dense woods had a narrow path. It lured him in. As he strolled through the tall columns of trees, with their smooth and almost magically glistening bark, Armand eventually came upon a clearing. He stopped dead in his tracks!

Up ahead he saw an old man sitting at an easel, painting a mysteriously somber yet beautiful landscape. There was no mistaking it; the enigmatic canvas was in every sense the work of Jacob van Ruisdael, the 17th century Dutch master.

Silently, Armand walked up behind him and gazed down at the painting. "That's rather intriguing."

Michel jolted, then turned, shock marring his wrinkled face, as Armand wryly added, "It looks exactly like Jacob van Ruisdael's *Jewish Cemetery*, especially since I see no cemeteries or ruins in the Hudson Valley from here."

"You have quite an eye for the old masters, Mr.—?"

"Arnolfini, Armand Arnolfini."

"Arnolfini?" Michel queried in his thick Italian accent. "As in Jan van Eyck's *Giovanni Arnolfini?*"

"The very same, indeed, just several generations removed."

"My Lord, son. You come from a mighty famous family. Yet, I must confess, you look nothing like your ancestor, and thank heavens for that! You look rather healthy and alive."

"Yes, and my vision and sense of deduction is also quite healthy," Armand said as he glanced back at the canvas. "Do you intend to sign that Jacob van Ruisdael?"

Michel laughed. "You may be a famous Arnolfini, Armand, but I am not a van Ruisdael. Nor a Jacob, at that. I am just a nobody."

Armand smiled. "You are certainly not a nobody, Paolo."

Michel's lips twisted with confusion. "What do you mean by Paolo? My name is Michel, Michel Tucci."

"Nice try. But you, signore, are Paolo Santanello—a

phenomenal surrealist artist who, for some reason, remains an enigma."

Michel laughed, mockingly. "You, son, have a vivid imagination. How ever did you deduce such a fallacy?"

"I'm sure the names Bernard Higley, Clara Vandermeer, and Anton Platzer ring a few bells." Michel rolled his eyes, unimpressed, as Armand continued, "And quite oddly, Franz Liszt's *Second Piano Concerto* also aided in my deduction."

Michel's head recoiled, now totally confused. "A concerto!?" He then snickered with a condescending smile as he shook his head and slapped his leg. "You are most entertaining, Signore Arnolfini. But, please, do explain."

Armand remained stern and stoic. "Well, you see, Liszt had pioneered a very unique device. He launched his concerto with a single theme, which then underwent a series of transformations, at one point dark and brooding, and other times playful, dreamy, or even triumphant, but all emanating from that same single kernel. It made me realize that all these various old masterworks, which appeared to be by different Renaissance artists, were all by the same hand, the hand of a modern surrealist whose tantalizing works appeared underneath all of them. You, Paolo, are the kernel, the one theme that carried through the entire set, being brilliantly transformed only on the surface by masterful forgeries." Armand cracked a satiated smile as he peered deeply into the phantom forger's eyes. "So after contemplating all those loose ends, and now seeing you paint this picture, your name alone, Signore Santanello, ties them all together."

Paolo's frail shoulders wilted as his gnarly old hand laid the paintbrush down near his rich palette of oils. He expelled a sigh of regret mixed with relief. "It's been a long hard road, son, and I'm at the end of that trail. Life isn't always fair." His eyes veered toward the canvas then back up at Armand. "It has long been said that hard work and effort will reap great rewards. But I say, *bah!*" Paolo blustered with cynicism. "I had studied with intense vigor, Signore Arnolfini, perfecting my craft to the highest degree possible, yet met with one rejection after another by curators, snobs, and collectors of all sorts. I'll have you know, as a young lad, back in the early nineteen hundreds, I had created startling images of surrealism, even before those of Giorgio de Chirico. His now famous painting *Song of Love* had allegedly ignited the avant-garde genre of surrealism in nineteen fourteen, some ten years before André Breton *allegedly* founded the movement." Paolo shook his head with disgust. "How bizarre and flawed mankind is in documenting progress or ascribing credit."

Armand nodded, knowing well the flaws of recorded history. "I must admit, Paolo, although I have a personal interest in surrealism, my father and I have long been aficionados of the old masters, so my knowledge of surrealism's founding is not clear." Armand squinted. "But are you saying you actually pioneered surrealism before de Chirico?"

Paolo snickered. "My boy, as I said, life is not fair. Yes, I *did*. As a young man in nineteen eleven, at age twenty-two, my work was on display in an open market in Turin, Italy, my hometown. By an odd stroke of bad luck, Giorgio de Chirico happened to pass through my village on his way to Paris. Some three years later, I had seen a photo of *Song of Love* in a newspaper article, heralding de Chirico as a pioneer. That work—might I add—was very much like the one I had on display three years prior. Oh, yes, Signore

Arnolfini, I most certainly pioneered surrealism well before de Chirico, Dali, Ernst, Magritte, and the rest."

"I don't understand," Armand said. "If Giorgio and others were breaking new ground with their art, why did your attempts fail? Especially if your artwork was not only similar but the precursor."

Paolo swallowed hard as his wrinkled lips twisted. He looked up at Armand, his weathered and once vibrant brown eyes now reduced to two black pools of pain and sorrow. "My father had died in the Great War, and my mother's health spiraled into a deep state of melancholy. It was either abandon her and strike out into the world for self glory or retreat back into the womb of my existence, namely the warm and tender-loving arms of my mother."

Solemnly, Armand shook his head as his eyes drifted to the vast panorama of mountains and streams in the Hudson Valley, then back at Paolo's improvised van Ruisdael. "I'm still a bit baffled, Paolo. You have extraordinary talents. This van Ruisdael is just as magnificent as the other artists you copied with masterful skill, each in different genres no less. You mean to say you couldn't score a big hit, somehow?"

Paolo began packing up his materials as he said, "Armand, technical skills of imitation are not worth a damn. What makes a great artist great is their heart and soul, imagination and innovation. Anyone can acquire a wealth of knowledge, yet only those who utilize that knowledge in a unique and innovative fashion have earned the right to be called brilliant. These forgeries I have done over the years have all been cheap imitations. Painting restorers are a dime a dozen, and their names remain obscured and their financial rewards remain marginal. And in a sense, rightfully so. I missed my chance when I was young to make my mark. My mother lived for twenty more years after my father died, yet by that time World War Two had broken out and the world was not interested in buying art, as much of it was hidden or stolen. Especially by that fat bastard Hermann Goering! He was the world's biggest art thief."

Paolo stood up and folded his chair as he continued, "Fortune has not shone upon me in regard to my art, but did so with my heart. Those years with my mother, and the woman who had become my wife, were the pearls in the oyster shell that became my sheltered life. When they both died in a Fascist raid by Mussolini's henchmen, that's when I myself spiraled into a sad state of depression. It crippled me for a decade, until I decided to paint over my own creative canvases with forgeries of old masters to make a living, a *fair* living, one more in line financially with my worth. Great artists, Signore Arnolfini, deserve adequate compensation for the rich cultural enhancements they bequeath to civilization. Over countless centuries too many great artists, musicians, and even inventors have died penniless and forgotten, yet mankind has not made any attempts to correct this most humiliating and debilitating flaw."

Paolo cleaned his paintbrush carefully with turpentine and packed it neatly away with his linseed oil and special varnishes, as he added, "I have chosen to forge the works of lesser-known artists to keep a low profile and not incite a world-wide manhunt." He paused but a moment, then said reflectively, "However, I suppose I sold my soul to the devil, burying my love and passion under a veneer of falsehoods just to earn a fair living. Now I am ninety years old and the journey is almost over. Soon I shall cross the celestial threshold and return to my loving wife and mother's arms, and get to see my father once again."

Paolo handed Armand the painting and folding chair and collected his easel and paints. "Come, follow me."

They travelled back through the glaring birch trees and returned to Santanello's unique A-frame chalet, with his exquisite '37 Cord parked in the driveway.

Armand stopped. "Ah, yes. Now it all fits." He glanced at the priceless old Cord, then up at the modern chalet. "You cherish antiquity, but also modernity."

Paolo chuckled. "Very good, Armand. Yes, I most certainly do. I admire the old masters, but progress must be made. In fact, if you're wondering where I got all the old canvas fabric to paint my modern artwork, it was from my ancestor who owned a mill during the Renaissance. I had found reams of it in his attic and thought it would be interesting to paint modern visions on ancient canvas. Only later, when I began my charade, did I realize that my forgeries would be readily accepted when they examined the canvas from the back. Odd, how that, too, all worked out, as if destiny tried to throw me one small bone. But now it's over. *Finito.* So, please, follow me."

As they entered the chalet, Armand's eyes illuminated. There before him was a sprawling arrangement of paintings of all sizes by various artists, famous artists. Armand placed the faux van Ruisdael and folding-chair down and stepped closer to inspect *Aristotle Contemplating the Bust of Homer* by Rembrandt. He marveled over the light and dark brushstrokes that precisely imitated the great Dutch master. Then he stepped over and gazed at *The Crucifixion of Saint Peter* by Caravaggio. He stepped back and said, "Dear God, Paolo! I have studied the originals up close many times, and I must say, these are fantastic. I cannot tell the difference." He glanced at Paolo. "It's scary how mind-boggling your skills are. You have masterfully reproduced the works of two great titans who shared a very similar style."

Paolo approached Armand's side. "Yes, as I said, life is not always fair. For many years Rembrandt basked in the limelight because of his dramatic style of chiaroscuro, while Caravaggio—being the true pioneer of the style—remained in the shadows, forgotten for centuries. It's a crime to humanity." Paolo paused, then added, "Actually, in an odd way, it's sadly apropos, as their painterly style of light and shadow underscored their own disparate fates." He gazed up at Armand. "Wouldn't you agree?"

Armand shrugged. "Well, yes. But in recent years there's been a revival of Caravaggio's works. And now both great masters share the limelight. So, you see, Paolo, life sometimes corrects its mistakes, even if years or centuries later. After all, Mozart died and was buried in a pauper's grave. He, too, had fallen into obscurity for many years, having been blotted out by the huge shadow of Antonio Salieri. Yet Wolfgang rose from the ashes, like a phoenix, and has now cast Salieri into the shadows. So, genius often has a way of rising to the top."

Paolo's brief smile of acknowledgement turned into a frown. "Yes, but that some geniuses had to wait years or a century to be rediscovered is an awful tragedy. And who knows how many more Mozarts and Caravaggios have existed over time who will never see the light? There is much darkness in this world, much of which is borne in ignorance or sheer stupidity."

Armand stood silent and pensive, until several other canvases drew his attention; one by Renoir, another by Magritte, and still another by Holbein. "I thought you said you only painted forgeries of lesser-known artists?"

Paolo chuckled. "Well, these are copies of paintings I personally adore. I never had intentions of selling *them.*"

Armand examined them closer. "Are all of these painted over original creations of yours?"

Paolo's smile withered. "Yes. I suppose in a state of self-loathing, regret, or perhaps disgust, I have embarked on erasing myself from this cruel and unfair world." He gazed down at the van Ruisdael leaning against the wall. He expelled a deep breath, taking comfort in its significance, for the wet veneer of paint was slowly hardening, thus suffocating the last breath of the unknown surrealist underneath. "That is my swan song, Signore Arnolfini. I aptly chose van Ruisdael's gloomy landscape with a cemetery to vanquish my work, and inter my very self. I am now officially obscured from the eyes and minds of the unjust, the cliquey elites, the snobby academics, and the unfortunate public that shall never have a chance to judge my works for themselves." Paolo handed Armand a document that he had filled in while Armand was inspecting his collection.

Armand looked down and began to read it, when his eyes widened. His head snapped up, but it was too late, Paolo choked, wobbled, and collapsed.

Armand dropped the document and hurriedly knelt down by Paolo's side. Concernedly, he lifted the frail old man's head. His boney neck felt as if it might break, while his thin layer of skin seemed as if it might tear. "Paolo!" Armand cried as his heart raced. "Can you hear me?"

Paolo's eyes opened half way as he coughed and gurgled, while a rivulet of blood coursed down the side of his mouth. "Armand, I've managed to beat lung cancer for almost a year, but it's over. I have no family left. And who better to make the executor of all my wealth than an Arnolfini—a man with deep roots to a glorious artistic past. It appears destiny has brought you here, in this… final…hour, this…final—"

A painful lump welled in Armand's throat as he could feel the old man's body wilt and begin to stiffen—the warmth of a near century-long life slowly dissipating, as it ebbed into the cold abyss of death.

A tear welled in Armand's eye as he sat speechless, gazing at the old artist, then peering at the gallery of pseudo old masterpieces that extinguished a genuinely great, but unknown, modern artist.

Armand leaned back and once again gazed at Paolo's will. Not only did Paolo authorize Armand to be his executor, but Santanello had also left several millions of dollars to be dispersed to numerous art academies, which would be awarded as scholarships to promising young talents; budding artistic geniuses who exhibit the prospect of uplifting civilization in one form or another.

Once again Armand peered down at the mysterious phantom forger in his arms. He had vigorously hunted him down with contempt, only to find himself saddened and burdened with a heavy heart and conflicting thoughts. The dead old man before him was clearly a genius in his own right, but by the twisted forces of fate had been dealt a bad set of celestial cards. His mission of gaining financial compensation was not borne out of self-interest or greed, but rather a philanthropic endeavor to right the injustice of an often cruel and imperfect world, a world that routinely overshadowed or even trampled over many with extraordinary talent, either due to roadblocks by haughty elites, a lack of connections, a depletion of profits by greedy capitalists, or simply bad karma.

That Santanello had also made a life-long decision to literally erase his art, and in essence himself, from the world of art also struck Armand hard. A tear unexpectedly escaped from his eye and streamed down his solemn face. Yet as he gazed up at all of Paolo's forgeries, and contemplated all the press his monumental crime would soon engender, another thought struck him: will Santanello's surreal under-paintings now be revealed, thus being his passport into the pantheon of the ironclad-world of Fine Art?

Armand Arnolfini wiped the tear from his eye, and smiled.

THE RUSSIAN LINK

Armand Arnolfini's yellow 1937 Cord Coupe purred as he drove down Madison Avenue. He had inherited the classic quarter-million-dollar automobile from Paolo Santanello two years earlier, in 1978, after Armand had solved the now famous Phantom Forger case. Oddly enough, after Santanello's death, his surreal artwork had hit the world by storm, catapulting his name into the ranks of Dali, Magritte and the ultimate masters of surrealism, with his works fetching tens of millions of dollars or more at Christie's and Sotheby's. Beyond the exotic car, Santanello's estate entitled Armand to a five-percent royalty for the sale of Paolo's artwork; hence Armand's financial situation had been significantly augmented.

Arnolfini's notoriety of being a top-notch private investigator had also escalated since then, but it was now Sunday evening and his day to relax. As he made a hard right onto 57th Street, he ejected his cassette of Pink Floyd's new double album *The Wall*. As he came to a red light he slipped the cassette into the rack on the center console. "All right, I think I'm comfortably numb enough. Time for a little Russian roulette."

He gazed at the cassettes of Russian composers in his Classical section, and randomly ran his finger over the names of Stravinsky, Rachmaninoff, Rimsky-Korsakov, Prokofiev, Shostakovich, Khachaturian, and finally stopping on Tchaikovsky. His eyes widened as he contemplated how prophetic the selection was. "Ah, great choice!" he said, as he thought: *Then again, you can't go wrong with any of these darn Russkies.*

Darn, not because Armand didn't like Russians, it was only the political and military thugs he loathed, who turned their nation into an aggressive and oppressive machine, intent on devouring other nations. Unfortunately the Cold War had been escalating. Just recently, in response to the USSR's invasion of Afghanistan last year, President Carter had imposed a grain embargo. However, some of Armand's friends in the FBI, where he used to work, had ominous feelings about Afghanistan and the Middle Eastern region in general.

Nevertheless, as the light turned green, Armand stepped on the accelerator and slipped in the cassette. The Bose speakers ignited as the deep brooding strains of Tchaikovsky's *Manfred Symphony* oozed out. As he passed the Russian Tea Room, he couldn't help but think how so many Americans only knew Tchaikovsky for his famous and fanciful ballets, never having the good fortune of hearing his vast output of stunning symphonic poems, symphonies, and concertos that overflowed with unbridled passion and innovation.

He passed Carnegie Hall and turned south on 7th Avenue, then east on 56th Street, where he pulled into the parking garage. Hank, the garage attendant, ran to the distinctive '37 yellow Cord and opened the door. "Good evening, Mr. Arnolfini. The usual?"

"Yes, Hank, keep my beautiful canary safe. I'll only be two hours or so."

As Armand exited the exotic car, Hank hopped in and carefully parked it right next to the front office in a special stall surrounded by stanchions with red velvet ropes.

Armand entered Carnegie Hall, handed in his guest pass, and found his seat in the orchestra section, third row from the stage. An usher walked past and handed him a Playbill, which Armand eagerly opened. It was the hundred and fortieth anniversary of Tchaikovsky's birth and the gala tonight not only was featuring a fine selection of his music, but was premiering a display of artifacts and paintings related to the great Russian composer.

With a cacophony of discordant sounds, the orchestra readied themselves as they warmed up. Center stage was the massive black Steinway that Horacio Juarez would soon be manipulating, whereby luring the audience into the mind and genius of Tchaikovsky via his *Piano Concerto No. 1*.

Walking on stage to a welcoming round of applause was Andre Lamont, who mounted the podium, took a bow, and turned toward his talented assemblage of musicians. Once silence was obtained and the lights dimmed, Andre glanced at Horacio, who nodded, thus signaling the green light to commence.

With a swipe of his hand, Andre's baton launched the concerto. The orchestra punched out its eight introductory blasts when the lush iconic melody took over and sang its majestic tune. Some thirty-five-minutes later, the masterpiece reached its conclusion, as the audience applauded. Soon they wriggled in their seats, stretched their legs and, of course, coughed—vehemently.

Armand rolled his eyes. He had always found it odd how people only seemed to cough when classical music was played or during intermissions. He often thought that if people coughed like that in restaurants there'd be federal health laws passed requiring all patrons to wear facemasks, as not to contaminate other people or their meals. So how was it, he thought, that they only coughed like Flu victims in performing arts centers?

Armand shifted irritably in his seat, hoping the coughing would not ruin the next piece, which happened to be the symphonic poem *Romeo and Juliet*. Quite inexplicably, as Andre Lamont raised his hands, the hacking and coughing miraculously stopped.

Armand smirked. *So they* can *control their coughing!*

Meanwhile, the astute conductor took advantage of the brief moment of silence, as he quickly launched the piece. The soft and mesmerizing opening—riddled with sad undertones—brilliantly foretold the violent clashes of familial conflict and heartache that was soon to come. Building into a crescendo, the music exploded, as the full orchestra pounded out its fury, then slowly subsided, as a soft, romantic melody emerged from the storm. Armand sighed and slouched in his seat, breathing in its charm and beauty, when suddenly he heard an annoying *pop!*

He sat upright as his head spun, trying to locate the direction of the irritating sound. He glanced at the middle-aged woman sitting to his right, who merely shrugged her shoulders, then turned to his left. The elderly man next to him seemed not to notice or even care about the bothersome sound.

But then there was another *pop!* And another!

Andre Lamont pivoted around, at first annoyed, but as the audience began standing up, nervous and confused, Lamont briskly waved his hands, thus silencing the orchestra.

Someone yelled from the rear, "There's been a shooting!"

As panic set in, people dashed toward the exits. Armand jumped up and plowed his way through the hysterical crowd. Making his way into the lobby, he noticed everyone filing out the front and side doors. He made an about-face and headed down the corridors to the rear of the building. He came upon the manager, Oliver Whittaker, who gazed at Armand with petrified eyes. Swallowing hard, Oliver tried to bury the sorrowful sight he had just witnessed to greet his friend. "Arnolfini! I'm glad you're here."

"What happened?"

Oliver turned and pointed to the dead body on the floor. "That's Michael, my stagehand. He tried to stop the thief, but, but now he...he's d-dead." As he replayed the horrific memory in his mind, Oliver filled with rage, as he spat, "The brutal t-thug first carved him up with a dagger, then, after cursing him out in German, shot him t-three times. Three times! He's an animal! An utter animal!"

Armand compassionately grasped Oliver's shoulder. "Calm down, take a breath." He then noticed the dagger on the floor. It was a Nazi SS dagger. Armand walked over and looked at it closely. "Hmm, it's the real deal," he said. He turned back toward Oliver. "What did the thief take, and where did he go?"

Oliver glanced at Armand, still dazed and numb, as he tried to collect his thoughts. "Uh, well, he s-stole a painting, Armand, our prized *Tchaikovsky Memorial*, no less.

It's by Silvio Riccadella. Quite exquisite and expensive." He paused briefly as he glanced back at the corpse of his young employee, then continued, "Evidently the animal stuffed it into a valise, which had a small eagle emblem on it, and ran out the rear entrance." Oliver pointed with his shaking finger. "Over there!"

"Call nine-one-one," Armand said commandingly, "I'm going after him!"

As Armand dashed toward the rear exit, Oliver called out, "But he still has a gun! Let the police handle this."

"No time to lose!" Armand exclaimed as he exited.

Armand ran into the street and saw a 1976 tan Mercury Cougar XR 7 tearing out.

An old feeble man was sprawled out on the curb; his groceries splattered all around him. Angrily, he gazed up at Armand. "Who the hell was that moron? That crazy fellow knocked me over and just took off!"

Armand helped the old man to his feet. "Are you all right? I mean hurt in any way?"

"Just my pride, son. You expect a little respect when you get my age."

"Well, I'm glad you're not hurt, but I have to run." As Armand took off toward the parking garage, he heard the old man call out, "Run where?"

"After that moron!"

Armand pulled out his extra set of keys and dashed to his '37 Cord. As he hopped in, he yelled out to Hank, "I'll square away with you later!"

The hide-away headlights of the old classic flipped open, looking like a sleeping dragon that awakened, with eyes blazing, while the Firestones burned rubber and the car lunged into the street.

Armand chased the red taillights of the tan Cougar, weaving between cars as best he could. The Cougar sped up and made a mad dash for the Queensboro Bridge, speeding through the intersection and onto the ramp. Armand pushed the pedal to the floor and tried to follow, but the Cougar had caused a large Mack truck to collide into two cars, which now blocked the entrance ramp.

Armand applied the brakes and cut the wheel hard right, now heading south. His mind reeled: *If this old-time Nazi stole a painting, I'll bet ten to one he's heading back to the Fatherland.* His eyebrows lifted. *Of course, JFK Airport.*

Armand raced down to the Midtown Tunnel, then made a beeline to the airport. Armand's fingers dug into the steering wheel. *I hope to God I'm right,* he thought. At this point, Armand felt he had nothing to lose; the Cougar had escaped him.

He pulled into the airport and coasted into the Long Term parking lot. He came to a stop and shut off the engine and lights, which retracted back into the fenders. His eyes surveilled the airport but saw no sign of the killer/thief. His hands tapped the steering wheel, anxiously, as his mind sank into a pool of doubt. He gazed at his watch. It was 9:36 PM. As each second and minute ticked closer to failure, Armand's vengeful fingers dug deeper and deeper into the steering wheel.

His mind reeled: *You dirty bastard, you couldn't just punch the stagehand; no, you had to mutilate the poor kid and then shoot him. Three times!* Armand shook his head. *Are you just a crazy American Neo-Nazi or the real deal?*

Twelve minutes passed. Armand glanced at his Rolex and huffed, dejected. *I couldn't have beaten him here by twelve minutes. Damn it, my guess was...*

Armand's eyes widened!
Right!

Just then the 1976 tan Mercury Cougar turned into the Long Term parking lot at the adjacent terminal. Armand slipped out of the Cord and ran feverishly toward the Cougar as it pulled into a stall. Armand's sprints and stamina from his days of playing professional soccer had evidently not waned, as he zeroed in on his target, who was wearing a brown, army-style jacket and was just now exiting his car. Armand threw the first punch, but soon fists were thrown and grunts echoed in the night air. The thug's mean gnarly face twisted as he reached for his pistol, but Armand, with lightning speed, head butt him while simultaneously clipping his ankle with an illegal soccer move that he reserved only for creeps, whereby causing the thug to fall flat on his back.

Armand adroitly snatched the pistol and pushed the barrel into his face. "Who the hell are you?"

As the thug squirmed, Armand pushed his knees deep into his biceps while his left hand clasped the killer's throat like a vice grip.

The man's lips twisted with animus as he replied in a deep, German accent, "You *will* regret this. I swear!"

"No, *you* will regret mutilating a young man in cold blood and stealing a valuable painting!"

"Go ahead, kill me! I will *not* talk!" the murderous thief growled.

Armand eased up on his stranglehold and stood up, still pointing the gun at the animal's face. "Get up! Give me the valise with the painting. And if you make any silly moves, I *will* kill you!"

The man snickered. "You Americans can't kill anybody. You have laws, stupid laws that protect guys like me."

Armand cocked the hammer back. "Well, you don't know *guys like Me!*"

The man uneasily rose up to his feet while his hand slipped into his pocket and retrieved something. What it was, Armand couldn't tell, especially in the dark parking lot, yet the thug slipped the item into his mouth and bit down hard. Before Armand could process what happened, the thug fell to the ground as foam oozed out of his mouth—the toxic cyanide poison suffocating everything in its path as it raced through his veins. The writhing was extremely brief, as four violent convulsions and a final guttural gasp signaled the end of his life.

Armand recoiled in shock. *What the hell is going on? Suicide?* He glanced around the dark parking lot. No one was in sight. Some eighty yards away, the hustle and bustle of taxis, buses, and cars picking up or dropping off travelers continued without a hiccup, while Armand's poor brain was blindsided by a flurry of hiccups. It was like his mind was a strobe light, blinking rapidly as flashes of different options bombarded his senses.

He reached down and opened the man's brown army jacket, then slipped out his wallet and flipped it open. His eyes squinted as he thumbed through the stack of West German Deutsche Marks, then widened as he slipped out a card that was hidden in a back compartment. It was old, yellowed and tattered. It was a Waffen SS card. It read Helmut Hein, SS-Untersturmführer.

Armand gazed down at the dead middle-aged man. He appeared to be no older than forty-five. Armand reached in and pulled out the dead man's passport and flipped it open. It read Helmut Hein. Armand huffed as he kicked the dead body. "What the hell were you trying to pull? You weren't old enough to be an SS officer."

He glanced around, realizing he spoke his thoughts out loud. *Shut up, Arnolfini! There must be a logical explanation.*

He searched through the wallet again, this time finding another card in the hidden compartment. It, too, was old and tattered, and read Helmut Hein II, Hitler Youth. *Ah ha! You sick little bastard. Like father, like programmed son.*

Armand then came across the dead man's airline ticket. Armand gazed at his watch. It was 9:55 PM and the flight was for 10:30 PM. Destination: Nuremberg, Germany. He tapped the documents against his hand, thinking. Suddenly he smiled, leaned down, and took off the dead man's army jacket and slipped it on. He gazed at the killer/thief's face, hair color, and body size, and despite the differences, figured he might be able to get past the airline clerk.

He didn't like disturbing a crime scene, but figured Helmut Hein might have been meeting his partner or an art collector at the Nuremberg Airport, so time was of the essence. He had to take the chance.

Armand retrieved the valise from the trunk of the Mercury Cougar and opened it up. There, inside, was the coveted painting by Silvio Riccadella, the *Tchaikovsky Memorial.* He couldn't help but admire the portrait of the famous Russian composer, which was embedded in a memorial featuring architectural aspects of St. Basil's cathedral and the Bolshoi Theater, with iconic symbols from Tchaikovsky's various ballets. He closed the case and straightened out his brown army jacket. He smirked, realizing it was a Hitler brown shirt replica, or more likely authentic. He made sure all his stolen documents and wallet were in order, then strolled into the Delta terminal and marched up to the check-in counter. With his head lowered, he handed his ticket and passport to the attendant, who fortunately was interrupted by her co-worker. The distracted attendant carried on her conversation, barely glancing at

Armand's documentation, and processed his papers. Armand turned quickly and began walking toward the gate when the attendant called out, "Excuse me, sir! I need to check-in your luggage."

Armand turned, and smiled. "No, thank you. It's a carry-on."

The attendant hadn't even noticed his appealing looks, but now smiled. "Have a nice flight," she said, as she turned back to her co-worker and giggled.

Armand sighed and kept walking.

Some fifteen hours later, Armand landed in Nuremberg at 7:30 PM. His hand was sweaty from holding the precious valise the entire flight, but as he deplaned and strolled into the terminal, his eyes intently surveilled the area. He walked slowly, hoping the art collector or partner would notice the valise with eagle insignia and approach him. What that person would say or do, Armand wasn't quite sure, but he knew the odds were great that someone there would recognize the prized valise or Helmut's Hitler-styled, brown-shirt army jacket.

He stopped to get a cup of coffee and a newspaper at the cafe and sat in the open lobby. With the valise under his arm, and the eagle emblem conspicuously displayed, he skimmed through the newspaper and sipped his coffee, as the fleeting minutes turned into two long hours. He groaned; he had waited long enough.

Armand pulled out Helmut's wallet and gleaned the home address on his driver's license, then hailed a taxi. As they drove through the quaint village of Nuremberg, with its narrow cobblestoned streets, Armand instructed the driver to pass the unassuming, yet now infamous, Kunstbunker.

The Art Bunker entrance was merely a set of two wooden doors with huge decorative hinges that was sandwiched between a line of apartments and shops on the village street of Obere Schmiedgasse. However, this vault was where the Nazi's had stashed precious works of art they had stolen during the war, along with historic artifacts from Germany, including works by Albrecht Dürer and the Royal Crown from the Holy Roman Empire. As they drove past, Armand surveilled the area, since he was well acquainted with the Art Bunker's notorious past. In fact, it was this Nazi hideout that solidified his hunch when he discovered Helmut's ticket to Nuremberg. As they drove on, Armand gazed up at the mountain behind the bunker, where he saw an impressive view of the old Imperial Nuremberg Castle. It was the spot where many had assumed the stolen art was stashed, but proved wrong.

The taxi finally arrived at Helmut's apartment, where Armand paid the cabby, pulled out Helmut's keys, and entered the flat. He placed the valise on the couch and opened it up once more to admire the prized painting. He was quite familiar with Riccadella's *Tchaikovsky Memorial,* as it had been reproduced on collector plates that retailed at performing arts centers in America and Europe. It was part of Riccadella's Pantheon of Composers collection, which featured several other great classical composers. Being a lover of the arts, Armand had collected several of Riccadella's plates himself, but there was nothing like looking at the original oil painting, with its vivid colors and intricate details.

Armand carefully shut the valise and leaned against it as he turned on the television. He gazed blindly at the TV screen, as his mind churned. *Why didn't someone approach me?* His baffled and weary mind conjured up a series of unanswered questions until his eyelids couldn't maintain the weight anymore, and he eventually nodded off, the jet lag taking hold.

The noises of the television changed from jovial commercial jingles to sappy sitcoms, then to serious news, when suddenly the door burst open! Before Armand could open his eyes, he felt a walloping thump and saw a bright flash of white light! The assailant had punched him square in the face. Instinctively, Armand raised his arms, and kicked hard! The assailant flew backward, landing on the floor. Yet as Armand regained his vision, he realized there were two thugs, as the other man, who was older, taller, and wearing a ten-thousand-dollar Kiton suit, reached for the valise. Armand grabbed the older man's wrist and twisted it inward, causing him to cave in by Armand's knees, whereby he wrapped his legs around the man's torso and pummeled him in the face, repeatedly, to a flurry of grunts and whimpers.

Meanwhile, the other assailant lunged at the entwined bodies and pried his older partner loose. Armand sprang to his feet, but the stocky young man pulled out a gun. "Move away from the valise, *mach schnell!*" he barked in broken English and German, as he wheezed from the earlier belly kick.

Armand took a step away from the couch.

Meanwhile, the older man pulled a handkerchief out from his classy suit and wiped the blood away from his split lips. He peered at Armand with his blue dagger eyes, as he slowly opened the valise. He gazed down at the painting, smiled, then shut the lid. He looked at his young cohort, "*Ja, es ist hier.*"

Armand brazenly stepped toward the older man; while the thug with the gun stepped behind Armand, and barked, "Don't move!"

Armand faked a punch, then kicked the older man square in the chest. As he fell backward, Armand did the unexpected. He used a Pelé bicycle kick to clobber the thug behind him! Before the brute knew what happened, Armand had already been rotating upside down when his foot smashed him in the face. Armand's soccer stunt had changed the whole dynamics, as he bent over and retrieved the fallen revolver. As the two Germans wobbled to their feet, Armand pointed the pistol at them and said, "Okay, I enjoyed the tussle, but the game is over. Who the hell are you?"

Both men looked at one another, humiliated, then back at Armand. The older one, in the Kiton suit, snarled, "Never mind who we are, where is Helmut?"

The younger man, who was evidently the older man's henchman, remained silent.

Armand grasped the valise as he kept the gun aimed in their direction. "Your buddy, Helmut, is dead. Cyanide. Which tells me one thing, this operation of yours is extreme. And I'm talking about Nazi *fanatical* extreme."

The older man smiled condescendingly. "Nazis? Really? It is nineteen eighty. There are no Nazis left, you fool."

"I wish that were true, but Nazis are still being hunted down. Just a few years ago, Hermine Braunsteiner was found in Queens, New York. She was one of your evil, demented guards at Ravensbruck. She'll be going to prison, just like you two Nazi thieves."

Again the elderly man smiled and shook his head. "You have it all wrong. We are legitimate art dealers." He pointed to the valise. "And that painting, the *Tchaikovsky Memorial*, belongs to a Russian aristocrat. It was stolen from his collection and sold to the Carnegie Institute in New York. We're simply trying to return it to its rightful owner."

Armand sniggered. "Yes, you're art dealers, who just so happen to carry firearms, break into Carnegie Hall, kill an innocent employee, and now bust into my apartment. There are things called laws, gentlemen. And I'm not talking about anti-Semitic laws, like your infamous Nuremberg Laws of nineteen thirty-five, which were supposed to protect the purity of your rich Aryan blood. They also allowed Hermann Goering to start imprisoning wealthy Jews and art dealers to confiscate their valuable collections. And let's not forget, during the war Goering looted art museums in France, Belgium, Italy, and elsewhere, whereby amassing over twenty thousand pieces of artwork, some of which were buried in the Kunstbunker, right here in town." Armand gazed at them with reproachful eyes. "So I imagine you're just a bunch of leftover Nazis who still deal in stolen treasure; artwork that has never been recovered, or like this *Tchaikovsky Memorial*, that I'm betting you stole to sell to this rich Russian client of yours."

The two men glanced nervously at each other, as Armand added sternly, "So I intend to make sure you both suffer in prison for the rest of your rotten lives!"

With that, the young henchman tackled Armand onto the couch, where they both struggled, until the gun accidently went off. The Nazi thug let out an awful grunt as he rolled to the floor and held his bloodstained chest. His hands couldn't seal the breach as blood spurted out between his thick fingers, spraying the carpet and furniture like a lawn sprinkler. The fatal wound had struck his heart, which continued to pump the crimson liquid, as he gasped and trembled. Within several unnerving moments, he was dead.

Meanwhile, Armand had already stood up and once more pointed the gun at the distinguished elderly man in the suit. "I didn't intend that to happen, but if you try anything stupid, you'll end up just like him, a bloody mess. And I wouldn't want to ruin that expensive suit of yours."

The man's lips twisted in humiliation as he glanced down at his dead henchman, then back up at Armand. In his thick German accent he said, "You're an American, you have no jurisdiction here."

Armand waved the pistol. "*This* is my jurisdiction. But I happen to be Armand Arnolfini, a private investigator with strong ties to the FBI and Interpol, so either way, I *will* get what I want."

The man paused a moment, weighing his limited options. Then with a sigh, his once proud shoulders wilted. "My name is Herr Gerard Hoffmann. What exactly is it that you want?"

"I want the truth."

Gerard swallowed a lump of malice. "Well, you were partially correct, Mr. Arnolfini. Our Russian client is Boris Valdoff, a very wealthy man, with historic roots. He wants the *Tchaikovsky Memorial* for his personal collection, as he naturally has an affinity for all things Russian. But you were wrong about one thing. We are not Nazi remnants or art dealers, Mr. Arnolfini. We merely work for clients such as Boris, who deal in priceless stolen art and forgeries on the black market. He is the kingpin, the billionaire. His network is vast and would yield great returns for the art world if captured. Now the question I ask you is this: If I tell you where Valdoff is, will you let me go?"

"I think I can manage something, but you must personally take me to him, and—" Armand waved the pistol, "no funny stuff!"

"Agreed," Gerard replied. "He is in Stuttgart. It is only two and a half hours from here. We can take my car, if that's agreeable?"

"Sure, as long as it's not an Aston Martin with an ejector seat!"

Gerard cracked a halfhearted smile as he arrogantly shook his head. "You Americans and Brits are one crazy lot."

"Indeed we are, but not one millionth as crazy as you Super-*Stupid* Aryans."

Gerard's lame smile flipped into a scathing frown. "In that case, I'm rather disappointed. My car is only a Mercedes-Benz. No ejector seat."

"Okay, enough small talk, let's go!" Armand demanded.

Some two and a half hours later, they arrived at the Althoff Hotel in Stuttgart. Gerard Hoffmann had previously called Valdoff and arranged to meet at the hotel to make the exchange. Armand had instructed Gerard that he would pose as his new partner, Albrecht Schumann, and would have the pistol in his pocket, aimed at *him*, so no mishaps would be tolerated.

They now walked up the spiral set of stairs, and down the hall to room 256 to meet Valdoff. As they entered the suite, Boris greeted them with a welcoming grin, "Ah! Herr Hoffmann, so good to see you." Then peering at Armand, his jovial cheeks wilted with suspicion. "And you, I am told, are Herr Schumann, his new partner, *da?*"

"Yes, but please call me Albrecht. After all, we are all friends here. Right, comrade?"

Valdoff cracked a smile. "Naturally, comrade. Friends! Yes, friends!" he said as his lustful eyes glanced at the coveted valise in Armand's hand.

"Oh, yes," Armand said. "I'm sure you're very eager to see the *Tchaikovsky Memorial*." He placed the valise on the table. "Allow me," he said as he opened the lid.

Valdoff stepped over and lifted the artwork up, gently, scrutinizing the brushstrokes, then extending it backward to admire the entire composition. "Magnificent!

Truly brilliant," he said in his thick Russian accent. "We must celebrate!" he added, as he gently placed the artwork down. Then brutishly, he grasped a bottle of Stolichnaya Vodka, filled three glasses, and handed one to Gerard and another to Armand. *"Tebe!"* he cheered.

As they each returned a verbal salute and took a sip, Armand kept one finger on the trigger of the pistol in his pocket.

Evidently, Boris Valdoff had several vodkas before their arrival as he felt no pain, and for the benefit of Herr Schumann, he launched into a lengthy monolog about his family's royal roots and prestigious past. "I must tell you, Albrecht. I am a very important man. I am related to Catherine Pavlovna of Russia. Have you heard of her?"

Armand shook his head as he kept an eye on Gerard and took another small sip of vodka.

"Well, comrade, Catherine happens to be the Russian link, which married me, if you will, to my fellow Germans. You see, in the nineteenth century, Catherine had wed King William I of Württemberg. Württemberg, as you may know, includes this city. And it is here, in Stuttgart, where King William had the magnificent Württemberg Mausoleum built in her honor. Both monarchs are buried there." Boris staggered slightly as he walked to the window and drew back the curtain. "See, l-look there," he said with a slight slur. "On the mountaintop. Isn't it m-magnificent?"

Armand gazed out the window at the distant structure, which majestically mounted the peak. "Yes, it is marvelous."

Boris spun around to face his guests. "So, you see, Albrecht. It was my Russian family's connection to Germany, love of collecting and looting fine art, and my loathing of Stalin that made me partner up with Herr

Hoffmann and—" Boris cut short his revealing tale upon seeing Gerard discreetly shake his head with piercing eyes.

Armand caught the exchange, stepped back two paces, and pulled the gun from his pocket. Valdoff's eyes widened as his ruddy face filled with rage. "You deceitful wretch!" he screamed as he unexpectedly charged Armand.

Armand smashed Boris in the face with the pistol, then quickly grabbed his neck with one hand and tripped him with his foot. Boris fell face-first, hitting his head on the corner of the end table and falling unconscious to the floor. Before Gerard could make a move, Armand cocked the revolver. "Don't even think about it! You see what happens when half-wits mess with me."

Gerard stood motionless and mute, as Armand felt Valdoff's neck for a pulse. "The drunken Cossack will be fine. But you *won't be* if you don't cooperate." Armand stood erect and queried sternly, "Where are you stashing all the stolen art? Is it back at Nuremberg?"

Gerard remained silent, as Armand added, "Or is it right here, in Stuttgart?"

As Gerard's face twitched, Armand smiled. "Of course it is." He turned and looked out the window. "In the beautiful Württemberg Mausoleum." Gazing back at Gerard, he demanded, "And you're going to take me there!"

He reached down and extracted Valdoff's keychain from his pocket. "I imagine one of these will do the trick. Unless of course, you have the key?"

"As I told you," Gerard finally spoke. "Boris is the kingpin. I have no idea where he stores his stockpile of art."

"Sure you don't. You're just an innocent pawn in this whole scheme. You must think I'm a chump," Armand blustered. "Your buddy Helmut had an SS dagger that he used to mutilate a young stagehand. He was also a brown shirt, a Hitler Youth fanatic, who even committed suicide, like your cowardly Führer. And my guess is that you were part of the Kunstshutz, the Art Protection squad that protected works of art. Or should I say, '*looted* works of art.'"

Once again, Gerard remained stubbornly silent and stiff as steel.

Armand grasped the valise and pointed the gun at the Nazi's head. "Now move!"

Traveling in Gerard's Mercedes, they drove up the winding roads of the mountain and finally arrived at the peak. Standing before them was the impressive burial chamber. Built after the archetype of all domed buildings, namely the Pantheon in Rome, the Württemberg Mausoleum was a circular domed structure with three porticos and an entrance, which sat atop a flight of stairs decorated with four large urns mounted on pedestals.

Armand left the valise in the car's trunk and motioned to Gerard to walk in front of him. As they entered the majestic edifice, Armand was struck by the size of the mausoleum's interior, for it had previously been used as a Russian Orthodox Church up until 1899, and has remained in use to annually celebrate the Pentecost.

Armand spun his head around to look at the stunning, all-white interior, with its large coffered dome, adorned with rosettes, then down at the circular walls with columns, and finally landing on the iconostasis, decorated with oil paintings of various saints. "Very beautiful," Armand said. "But I doubt those six paintings account for the lucrative stash you have stored here." He turned toward Gerard. "So, where are they, Herr Hoffmann? Or do you prefer that I call you by your SS rank? After all, I wouldn't want to insult a high-ranking Nazi officer, now would I?"

Gerard's lips and slick eyebrows twisted with venom,

not appreciating the sarcasm. "Yes, at this point, you might as well show me some respect, Mr. Arnolfini. I am SS-Gruppenführer Hoffmann. I was one of Goering's most trusted and efficient group leaders, and did indeed head his Kunstshutz division. You are quite clever, Mr. Arnolfini. But for the record, we amassed more than twenty-*two* thousand works. We had works by Degas, Vermeer, Da Vinci, Raphael, Matisse, and many more!" He took out his white handkerchief and wiped the saliva from his heated lips, then added, "And yes, Boris was a buffoon! a spoiled, silver-spooned mediocrity who inherited massive wealth and never worked a day in his drunken, miserable life. He would have blown his entire family's fortune if not for me!"

"Very impressive, but I'm not impressed," Armand retorted as he aimed the gun at his head. "Now show me where you hid all the artwork."

True to form, the SS-Gruppenführer remained rigid as a rifle, arrogant as an Aryan, and stubborn as an SS-mule.

Armand smirked as he lowered the gun, while his eyes scanned the circular interior of the mausoleum. Then they gazed down at the large, wrought iron circular grating at the center of the brown, checkered-tiled floor. "Naturally," he said, "it must be in the crypt below. After all, your rabid mole, *Der Führer*, had a penchant for subterranean bunkers." Armand noticed the thick wooden door with a large padlock. He pointed the gun at Gerard, once again. "Let's go! That must be the entrance."

As they approached the large door, Armand pulled out Valdoff's keychain and inserted one key after another until it unlocked. He instructed Hoffmann to walk in front of him, down the dark steps into the crypt below. The curved-block walls and narrow stairs spiraled downward into an even darker and smaller stairwell that Armand was finding visually oppressive and unsettlingly claustrophobic. As they arrived at the lower level, light from the circular grating above shed a faint glow on the center of the floor, as well as on William and Catherine's tomb across the expanse. Armand looked around the circular chamber; he didn't see any paintings or doors. "Okay, Gruppenführer Hoffmann, where's the access panel?"

Again, Hoffmann remained militantly mute.

"My offer still stands, Gerard. If you help me, I'll do whatever I can to mitigate your case."

The Gruppenführer laughed disdainfully. "As you can see, Mr. Arnolfini, I am not a young man. And as they say, I was not born yesterday. You will not be able to mitigate my sentence, for as I told you; I am the mastermind of this operation, not Boris Valdoff. As such, Interpol and the German government will want my head."

Armand wanted to smash him *in the head,* but knew the loyal and obedient Nazi would never talk. His eyes scrutinized the dark interior of the crypt and spotted two statues, each in niches. One was of Moses and the other Mary Magdalene. Armand smiled as he stepped toward the statue of Mary, while still keeping his revolver aimed at Gerard's head. He noticed that the niche around the statue had an open seam. He grasped the statue with his free hand and pulled. As he anticipated, the entire niche with statue swiveled outward, revealing a steel door with a lock. Once again, he used Valdoff's keychain and managed to unlock the door.

Gerard nodded. "*Impressive.* Good guess, or perhaps just luck."

Armand smirked. "It wasn't luck, Gerard. No anti-Semitic Nazi would choose Moses. He freed the Jews. You morons cremated them."

"And thank God we did!" the Gruppenführer spat.

Armand smirked. "What did you Nazis know about *God*? Other than being his fallen angels."

Gerard hissed. "God himself used brimstone and fire to eradicate the wicked, Mr. Arnolfini! We knew well what had to be done."

"Yes, He did, but your brimstone and fire *backfired*, burning and razing Nazi Germany to a pile of rubble and dead carcasses. Many of your remaining leaders were round up and hung or committed suicide. It worked out *divinely*. Now, shut the hell up!" Armand flipped on the light switch, which illuminated a set of stairs that led into another chamber below the crypt. He pointed the gun at Gerard and instructed him to walk down first, as he followed. The damp musty air was oppressive and nauseating until they reached another steel door below. As they entered the chamber it was clear that the air temperature and humidity were precisely controlled. Armand's eyes widened in awe!

There before them, was a stash of over fifty works by various masters, such as Rembrandt, Rubens, Degas, Monet, Bouguereau, Gerome, Dou, Caspar David Friedrich, and among others, a Vermeer.

Armand walked slowly past the paintings, savoring each glorious vision. "Now, *this* is what I call *impressive*, Gerard." He eventually stopped at the Vermeer, glanced at the work, then gazed back at Gerard. "But this one is *not* so impressive."

Gruppenführer Hoffmann squinted. "What do you mean *not* impressive!? It's *Christ with the Woman Taken in Adultery* by *Vermeer*, perhaps one of the most valuable acquisitions Hermann Goering ever acquired."

Armand chuckled. "Gerard, I happen to be an aficionado of art, especially from the Renaissance to Baroque periods. And I also know the amusing history behind this particular piece."

Hoffmann's face radiated contempt. "What do you mean *amusing*?"

"I know very well that Hermann Goering traded one-hundred-and-fifty paintings he had looted, each by lesser-known artists, to acquire this Vermeer. But it's a fake! It's by forger Han van Meegeren. Your infamous fat man was duped!" Armand started laughing, while Gruppenführer Hoffmann gritted his teeth. "So, you know your art history very well, Mr. Arnolfini. But for your information, I was on the threshold of selling that fake for a sizable sum to an ignorant private collector. Namely, Boris Valdoff."

"Well, I'm sorry to ruin your lucrative racket, Gerard, but like your flamboyant master, Hermann Goering, it's time to head back to Nuremberg to stand trial for your sins." With that Armand pointed the pistol at his head. "Let's go, up the stairs!"

Gruppenführer Hoffmann's face radiated disgust as it turned crimson red. "I will *not* be humiliated by my *inferiors*!" he blasted. With a swift blur, Gerard pulled a cyanide capsule out of his pocket, popped it in his mouth and bit down hard! Before Armand could react, the toxic ion poison surged through Gerard's body, suffocating his heart, nerves, and muscle tissues, causing violent seizures, and ultimately, an agonizing death.

Armand stood bewildered and pensive. He shook his head, not understanding the fanatical nature that grips some people. Moreover, the fact that Nazi fugitives still remain, hidden in various corners of the world, was a disturbing thought. But he was glad to finally put this reprehensible art ring to rest once and for all. Hitler and Goering were the two biggest art thieves known to mankind, and despite ending this repugnant remnant of the Reich, Armand wondered how many masterpieces the Nazis had stolen or maliciously destroyed that would never see the light of day again.

After spending several hours explaining to the Stuttgart police and Interpol the roles of Gerard Hoffmann and Boris Valdoff, who had awoken from his concussion, Armand returned to Nuremberg, where he explained the death of Gerard's henchman to the police. He then spent several hours speaking to the hospitable villagers, content in knowing that the malignant Nazi virus had in large measure been eradicated, and that the honorable and industrious Germans of the day had made a miraculous comeback into the civilized world, becoming one of the wealthiest and innovative of nations. Offering many of those he met his deepest hopes that they would be reunited one day with their East German kin, he then took a taxi to the airport and returned home, landing at JFK Airport.

He walked across the street into the Long Term parking lot and started up his classic '37 Supercharged Cord, then drove straight to Carnegie Hall. There he met Oliver Whittaker, where he told him about the Russian link, namely, the convoluted tale of how the *Tchaikovsky Memorial* had led to a Russian/German Mausoleum in Stuttgart and eventually to an old Nazi art scheme. The *Tchaikovsky Memorial* was placed back on display, as millions came from all over the world to celebrate the anniversary of Tchaikovsky's birth with first-rate performances and a dazzling display of rare artifacts and, of course, Silvio Riccadella's stylish painting, which now had a history-making tale of intrigue added to its resplendent aura.

A COURTROOM CALAMITY

I walked into the Traffic Court building for what was supposed to be a quick conference. Yes, a *conference* the letter stated, to review my traffic summons for driving while using a handheld electronic device.

I confess; I was merely changing a song on my iPod when the officer pulled me over last month. As I had told him, I was aware of not being allowed to use a cell phone while driving, but wasn't aware of this new "electronic device" law. So now just being seen with an iPod in your hand, even if it's not on or even functional, merits a summons. The rules have become so pervasive, profuse and complicated that it's now impossible for any citizen to keep up, or not to get snagged at some point for being involuntarily guilty of noncompliance. A perfect trap.

Along with these new laws we American citizens are now surveilled by Orwell's Big Brother, with cameras at traffic light intersections scanning our every move so they can nab and penalize us with excessive fines, which they sheepishly send via mail, not to mention how tolls now scan our EZ-passes, which electronically keeps tabs on our exact locations across the country. Why they just don't brand our forearms with numbers like the Nazis escapes me, yet that, too, may prevail soon enough.

Having lived long enough in this country, a disturbing thought becomes more real with every year that passes and with every new law inflicted on the public. From childhood we're inculcated to believe we are *free*, living in a democracy. Yet simultaneously we're brainwashed: slyly shackled into servitude, living in a police state that gets progressively more stringent and repressive. To believe otherwise is to live an illusion. Unconsciously, we submit to being slaves of an ever-intruding and oppressive system. Orwell's prediction has become manifest, and entering this building gave me the eerie feeling of being one of those subjugated drones in George Tooker's chilling 1956 painting *Government Bureau*. Both these artists perceptively foresaw where this was all heading, and I, along with millions of other indoctrinated inmates, am now a part of this gloriously deceptive prison without bars. At least no bars *yet*!

Anyhow, under my attorney's advice, I had mailed in my plea of guilty, being that this court is well known for not plea-bargaining electronic device tickets. Lo and behold, I received another letter stating that it was *mandatory* that I appear in traffic court. The Gestapo had spoken!

As I entered the lobby I was asked to remove all the items from my pockets, then was scanned by an overweight guard who evidently loved donuts, the glazed sugar lingering on his curly, French Cruller lips being a dead giveaway. I collected my belongings and was directed to go to the main conference hall, along with two hundred other offenders of the Reich. Fortunately we didn't have to be deloused before entering the chamber, nor did I see anyone tagged with a yellow Star of David, thank God.

I took a seat and waited as three processing agents called one name at a time to review their case. Naturally, out of the two hundred poor saps there, I was number 184 on the docket to be called. And, mind you, this was after waiting *three hours!* I walked up to the agent, who, without even looking at me, coldly reiterated my options; namely, to either set a trial date to dispute the charge—which I had already learned was futile—pay the fine and get 5 points on my license, or have a new, nifty Big Brother device installed in my car for three months to invade my privacy and scan my activity, perhaps even tabulating how many times I pick my nose. I mean, after all, picking one's nose *is* distracting, and God forbid you toss the nasal debris out the window, you'll be cited for littering. Okay, I exaggerate, but at least this monitoring device wasn't a microchip that would be surgically implanted. Then again, that, too, may only be months away in this United States of Anemia of ours, which, from my perceptive eyes, is becoming far more pale and sick these days. Or should I say, "sick*ening!*"

I shook my head in disbelief. "I don't understand," I said, "I was given the option to plead guilty with my initial summons in the mail, which I did. That should have resolved my case, yet I had to take off from work to come here and sit for three hours to hear what I already knew. Why is that?"

The agent, still gazing at his docket, sternly read out a long and impressive number—SP-17305489278 or something to that effect, which I assume was meant to intimidate me— as he obstinately asked again, "So, which option do you want?"

I felt invigorated! I was actually given the *freedom* of choosing an option. I jest, of course. I was getting annoyed. Yet I inquired, "So, if I opt to have you install this scrutinizing leech-device in my car, what's involved?"

The agent finally looked up at me and smirked. "You will need to come back here again to get it processed, then arrange for the installation."

"Ah, so another three hours waiting here, then arranging to get it installed, which I imagine will be another several hours. Bottom line, an additional full day or two that I need to take off from work with no pay. Is that about right?"

The agent rolled his mechanical eyes and smirked again. "Yes, I suppose so."

Now *I* smirked. "Fine. I'll take the fine. Let's just get this over with."

As I reached for my wallet, the agent stamped my documents and said, "Just take a seat and wait to be called."

I squinted. "Called for what? I just accepted the fine. Why can't I just pay for it right here and now?"

"That's not how things work around here. You must go before the judge. That's mandatory."

Ah, yes, that *mandatory* thing again. I smirked. "Yes, I see how things work around here, or at most government agencies. That's why politicians and legislators are paranoid about outsider business people taking their seats in government, because they know they'll look like fools when their inept system can be proven to work far more efficiently and cost effectively by others."

The agent's brow raised and his lips twisted, the first signs that told me the robot was actually humanoid, as he spat, "Take your seat, Mr. Hopkins!"

Now *I* rolled my eyes and took a seat. With my knees

bouncing in frustration and my eyes glancing at my watch, which ticked away another hour, I was at my wit's end.

Then the moment arrived; for the second time my glorious name was called out. The cheerless agent-robot pointed to another doorway as he declared in his cold, monotone voice, "Down the hall and to your right, go to Hearing Room C."

Eagerly, I marched to Hearing Room C and sat there with twenty other condemned souls. There we waited another thirty minutes to be called before the judge. When my name was finally called, I sprang to my feet and stepped up to the railing, which, thank God, was nicely marked with a sign that read "Stand Here," since without proper direction, I was about to sit on the stenographer's lap.

I kid.

The judge, like the previous drone I encountered, gazed down at the paperwork in his hands as he rattled off my lengthy-numbered violation and then enunciated the litany of charges with imperial gravity, "Your summons charge for driving while operating an electronic device, Mr. Hopkins, is two hundred and thirty-eight dollars, your driver responsibility fee is forty-five dollars, your public safety fee is fifty-five dollars, and your convenience fee is two dollars." He shuffled some papers, still without looking at me, and asked, "Do you plead guilty to this charge?"

I almost laughed. "Well, you listed *several* charges, so which charge are you referring to?"

The stenographer's eyes widened as her head recoiled, having anticipated a *one word*, Guilty, answer, while the judge's head snapped up from the documents in his hands with an irritable twitch. "Are you attempting to make a mockery of my courtroom, Mr. Hopkins?"

"Not at all, Your Highness, I mean Your Honor."

Before the judge could reprimand me, I continued, "I'm just confused, you mentioned several charges. And just what does your *convenience fee* account for? Inconveniencing *me* to take off from work to kill four and a half hours here?"

The judge slammed his papers down. "Your bad driving habits, Mr. Hopkins, are what's inconveniencing this court room and the taxpayers' money!"

"Well, Your Honor, if I was given a fair chance to defend myself, like back in the old days, you and the court would have found out that I haven't gotten a ticket in sixteen years and I haven't had an accident in over thirty-two years. So just how much of a driving menace and burden am I to my fellow taxpayers?"

The judge's gnarled face softened as he sat speechless for an odd moment, twirling the gold ballpoint pen in his hand. "Well...I don't *make* the laws, Mr. Hopkins, I only *interpret* them."

"Yes, I understand that we all fall into the rut of simply doing our jobs, but when do we stop and raise our heads to question some of these new laws or absurd policies?"

The judge leaned forward, irritated. "That is *not* within my purview, Mr. Hopkins. So I do *not* overstep my authority. But you've drifted well past the topic. I need a plea, Mr. Hopkins. You're wasting the court's precious time!"

"*I'm* wasting the court's time? I clearly responded to your summons in the mail and stated my plea of guilty, since my attorney informed me that no plea bargains are made for electronic devices. So whose time is being wasted? And for that matter, whose time is more valuable?"

The judge cringed. "I can easily cite you with contempt, Mr. Hopkins, and make this very painful for you!"

"Your Honor, this whole convoluted system is more painful than going through Dante's nine circles of Hell!" As everyone in the courtroom either gasped or chuckled, my cell phone vibrated. I gazed down to read the text as I continued speaking, "And while you may process people who violate increasingly stringent traffic laws, I happen to be a surgeon." I gazed up at the judge. "And I just missed a critical operation of a car accident victim. And that's all because of this ludicrous summons that could have been easily resolved through the mail."

Just then, a court attendant discreetly approached the judge and whispered in his ear, while I continued, "And I'm sad to say, Your Honor, the patient died."

The judge's face turned pale as the attendant apologized and exited the courtroom. "M-Mr. Hopkins," he stammered. "Or rather, Doctor Hopkins. Do you happen to work at St. Francis Hospital?"

I nodded. "Yes, I do."

"Was the patient's name Cathy Patterson?"

Now *I* squinted. "Yes, how did you…" I glanced at the judge's nameplate, which read 'Honorable George Patterson.'

The judge lurched forward as his trembling hands grasped his grief-stricken face. "Dear God! *No!*" he cried with a horrible shriek that could move even the heart of a heartless killer. With a tear-jerking whimper, he sobbed, "That…was my daughter."

TRAPPED

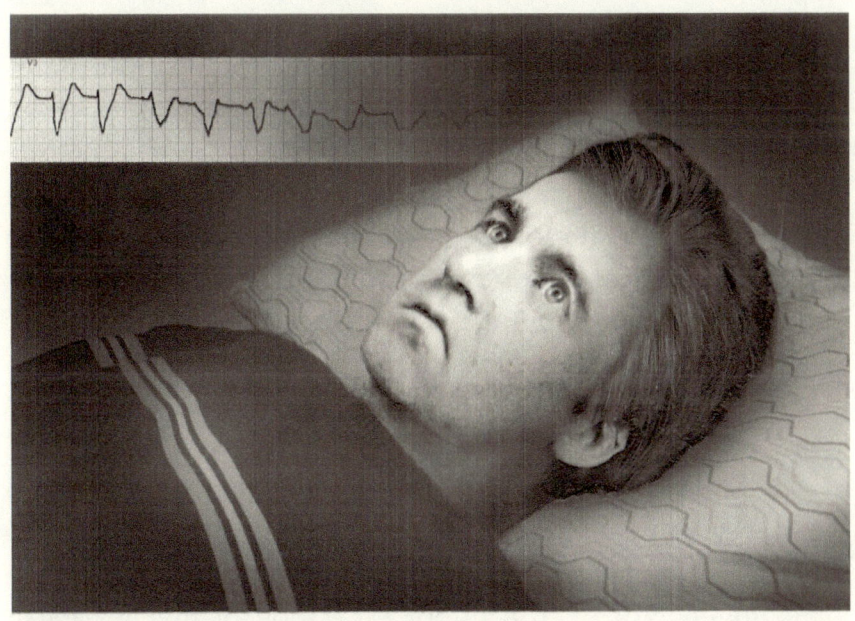

"Dear God!" I scream, panic-stricken. "*Please!* End this nightmare!"

Those same agonizing screams I have yelled for the past six and a half months, as I lay in a hospital bed in a deep coma, my screams unheard by the world outside my body, only echoing off the inner chambers of my tortured mind. I had been sentenced to this hellish prison for no fault of my own when a criminal broadsided my car; he had stolen a Ford Mustang, crashing into me while being pursued by police. Essentially, he also stole my life. The four others he had killed while holding up a convenience store were fortunate enough to die instantly, while I, for some unknown reason, was spared to endure this cruel and painful hell.

Meanwhile, friends and loved ones have hovered over my cadaver-like body for over half a year, chanting prayers or words of encouragement, like my dear wife, Catharine, summoning me now, "John, *please* wake up, come back to me!"

The tears that stream down my face are just illusions, only to be seen and felt in my tormented mind. I can even sense my throat tightening up with torn emotions, longing to answer my wife with the tender words, " I love you! I'm here!" Yet not a single word can she hear, nor does a single blip even ruffle the monitors. The pain I suffer is my own, unknown to every soul actively engaged in the beauties of everyday life, for I had lived a very energetic and prosperous life, one that has been heartlessly taken away from me.

Further compounding my curse is that I can see and hear everything, yet my body cannot even respond with the simplest of motor skills. Not even a slight twitch of the eye or a finger. Nor even a minor escalation of my heartbeat. Nothing! Nothing to let my loved ones or doctor know that I'm alive, at least mentally. My rigid body, now just a pile of useless tissue and bones, has become my tomb, locking me into this ungodly world of intangible consciousness, where I'm a mere ghost, a spectator of life. I have an active mind, still alive, vigorous, and healthy in every sense, yet it's shackled in a paralyzed and dormant body, a cage, a prison. I'm trapped!

No more can I run the New York Marathon, one I had placed third in last year. Nor can I scuba dive to see the beautiful coral reefs of the Pacific or ski the extreme slopes of the majestic Alps, all captivating pastimes of mine that are now reduced to vaporous thoughts, misty memories created by lightning-fast electrons and neurons traversing the synapses in my brain, the only signs that inform my doctor that I'm barely alive. Yet, even at that, the signals registering on the monitor must be flawed, plain wrong! They *must* be!

"I'm alive! Damn it! *Listen to me!*" I scream again, as I watch my doctor flick the monitor with his finger and shake his head, disappointed. "It's working fine, Mrs. Vagis. I'm so sorry," he says as he walks toward her and compassionately places his hand on her shoulder. "John's brain waves are the same as when we first admitted him over six months ago. So there's very little to give me hope that things will change. I think it's time to think of alternative options."

My eyes bulge with shock—in my mind's eye—as I see my wife's face turn from grief to animus as she replies, "Don't you *dare* give me that *alternative option* nonsense! This is not Nazi Germany where we kill the unhealthy or undesirables!"

I'm overwhelmed with pride at my wife's cogent response, as Dr. Bernstein recoils, removing his hand from her shoulder. "Mrs. Vagis, my father was one of the few survivors of Auschwitz. He saw what his fellow Germans were doing, even before the Final Solution, by killing off the sick, deformed, or just undesirable. But I'll have you know that the concept, and even the practice of euthanasia, was not born in Germany, but rather right in our nation's parent country, England."

As my wife's face turns from anger to curiosity, Dr. Bernstein pulls up a chair and sits down beside her. Taking a deep breath, he continues, "Euthanasia has a long and cloudy history, Mrs. Vagis, but in the modern sense, mercy killing has many roots, such as Britain's Herbert Spencer, who in eighteen fifty coined the expression 'survival of the fittest.' Nine years later, that was compounded by Charles Darwin's groundbreaking work on natural selection, giving many prominent people a reason to think it was best to eliminate the weak, the unfit, the undesirables."

As I watch my wife mellow to the doctor's compelling words, my humiliation subsides, being equally eager to hear Dr. Bernstein's historic tale of death.

"Meanwhile," he continues, "right here in America we had Samuel Williams, who, in eighteen seventy, argued for mercy killing in the event that a patient was terminally ill and suffering. These men were worlds apart geographically, yet oddly connected by streams of similar thought processes. A wave of advocates in America for euthanasia mushroomed with men like Robert Ingersoll, who in eighteen ninety-four advocated euthanasia for people dying of terminal disease, or Margaret Sanger, whose zeal for genetic control exceeded mere abortions. The most heinous being Charles Davenport, who was a genetic racist. So, even we have a long history with imposing death." As my wife's eyes broaden with amazement, Dr. Bernstein clears his throat and continues, "So as to your insinuation that the Germans introduced this concept, I can clearly say that the British had done the greatest amount of initial leg work to formulate and populate the concept, as they even founded a society in nineteen thirty-five called Dignity for Dying, which not only predated Nazi Germany's T4 program, but was advocated by such luminaries as H.G. Wells and George Bernard Shaw."

"I had no idea," my wife replies in a whisper, as the doctor compassionately nods, and continues, "Yes, most people don't know, Mrs. Vagis. While virtually everyone knows of Charles Darwin, very few know of his cousin, Francis Galton. Some have tried to demonize him for coining the term eugenics, but his philosophy was not evil. He sought to rid the world of sickness and pain via breeding of healthy species, to fast track his cousin's theory of natural selection, whereby only the strong and mentally sound of mind would thrive and survive."

"Dr. Bernstein," my wife replies. "My husband John *is* a man who is mentally sound and superior in many ways. As you know, he is a very successful man. And that mind, I believe, is still alive and well inside that rigid shell." As she glances at me, she adds, "We just need to help him come out of this epidermal straightjacket."

Feeling a surge of elation, I wish I could reach over and draw my wife in for a loving embrace, overwhelmed by her loyalty, love, and sagacious terminology, which I'm sure comes from her college days of being a biology major. Yet she had no need to utilize that knowledge, being that my early success afforded her a life of leisure and luxury. Something else I'm most proud of.

Meanwhile, Dr. Bernstein smirks as he glances at the floor and shakes his head. "Mrs. Vagis," he says in a voice deep with emotion, "John, I'm afraid, is gone. His brain waves indicate no signs of life, life as we know it for a human being, that is. I apologize if my suggestion seems coldhearted, but it's one born out of experience and one grounded in reality, given the unfortunate statistics we're confronted with. John has been completely unresponsive for over half a year, Mrs. Vagis. I understand how difficult it is to let go of a loved one, but how compassionate are you for holding on to him? Holding him back from going to rest, where he'll be free of this torment, this harrowing state of limbo that you, your family, and friends have endured for six ungodly months. Help me to help you, and John." Grasping her hand, he adds softly, "It's time. Let him go."

My immovable eyes strain to look at my wife as I see tears in her eyes begin to form. I feel my eyes also filling up, yet knowing it is only I who am aware of this un-seeable sensation, as if I'm in a distant dream world or another dimension, an ugly Twilight Zone, severed from reality. And in that dark and dreary moment, Dr. Bernstein's chilling words of facing reality hit me hard, so hard that the thought of my merciful death strikes me like a dagger to the heart. In pain, I gaze up and shriek, "Oh, Dear God! Is this what you have in store for me?" I can feel my body almost writhing with utter fear, despite the monitor's steady and almost flat-line reading of my vitals.

But my will to survive screams out in my mind, so loud it's deafening, "I DON'T WANNA DIE, GOD! *Please!* Break me out of this nightmare so I can embrace my precious wife once again, and prove this death dealer wrong!"

Yet my wife's head lowers, consuming the Death Doctor's words, as if a drug. Tears stream down her grief-stricken face, but then the unthinkable happens. She raises her head and nods. She nods!? "Dear God, what is she thinking," my mind screams in panic, as she replies, "Perhaps you're right, Dr. Bernstein. I concede."

I almost black out as the doctor pulls out papers from a folder and hands them to her to sign. As my beloved signs my life away, she looks up and adds, "Doctor, may I have a moment to say my last goodbye?"

"Of course," Dr. Bernstein says as he collates the papers and sticks them back into the manila folder. "I'll prepare the medication and be back in a few minutes."

I scream, "NO! STOP! I'm here, alive!" My internal eyes gaze at my wife. "Honey, don't listen to him! I can break out of this cocoon, I just need more time." Yet as Dr. Bernstein leaves the room my wife hovers over me and embraces me, tight. I can feel her warm breasts pushing up against my cool, stiff chest as her tears drip on my face. I long to rise up and kiss her, to fully embrace her as she sobs, gazing right into my rigid, doll-like eyes, while I look up at her gorgeous and steadfast face, at the woman who stood by my side through the bad times right up to the billion dollar life I carved out of this crazy world. My mind races, like my Lamborghini Veneno, as I silently cry, "Honey, I'm here! You must be able to feel something."

Yet the minutes pass like seconds, when Dr. Bernstein re-enters the room, the deadly vial in his hand. "Mrs. Vagis, are you ready?"

My wife kisses me on my rigid lips, then slowly stands up. She takes a deep breath and brushes the tears from her face, then utters in a voice torn with grievous affection, "Yes."

Again I shudder! My paralyzed eyes dart frantically at my wife, then at the executioner. "NO! You can't do this! My mind is alive, fully animated. You're an intelligent man, Doctor, you know what Descartes said, *'I think, therefore I am!'* I exist, damn it! You have no right to do this!"

As my wife steps aside, Dr. Bernstein walks over to my IV and inserts the vial.

Again I scream, "STOP! You must know that I'm alive!"

Yet I can feel the toxic drug surging through my veins. Like fire, it rips through my entire body, burning and scorching everything in its hellish path. I writhe in sheer agony as the sulfuric-acid-like drug assaults and terminates my organs one by one—which I can feel shutting down, as the serum works its way up from my pelvis, through my chest cavity, and now streams feverishly toward my brain.

I scream in terror! "NO! STOP! Please!"

But it's too late; the intrepid drug can no longer be controlled or withdrawn, as it invades my brain like a river of lava, scorching the stroma and connective tissues that melt in its fiery path. In agony, I can feel my precious mind—which had built a financial empire that only a handful of mortals could ever rival—begin to numb and deteriorate as my vision begins to fade, spiraling into an ominous void of bone-chilling darkness. In desperation I shriek, "Good God, N-NO! Plea…"

†††

Dr. Bernstein turns abruptly, shutting off the IntelliVue monitor to silence its disturbing, flat-line beep, then turns back, looking at Mrs. Vagis with solemn eyes. Respectfully, he places his hand on the corpse. "John is gone. You did the right thing, Mrs. Vagis. He's at rest, once and for all."

With a face torn with grief, Mrs. Vagis buries her head in the doctor's shoulder, as her nasal passage congests and tears once again break free. A polite embrace ensues for but a moment as she steps back and pulls a tissue from her Hermes Birkin bag. Wiping her nose, she asks, "What now?"

"Don't you worry, Mrs. Vagis, we'll take care of everything from here. All we need is the name of your undertaker. We'll prepare the body for them."

"Thank you, Doctor Bernstein," she says with a poor attempt to regain her bearing. With a last gaze at her husband, she turns and exits the room.

No sooner does she leave, than a man in a three-piece, gray Karako suit enters the room. He spins around to watch Mrs. Vagis walk down the hall and enter the elevator. Turning back toward Dr. Bernstein, he asks with a whisper, "So, did you swing it?" while trying to peer behind the half-drawn curtain.

Dr. Bernstein sighs with a discreet smile. "Yes, Bill. And thank God!" He closes the door and the two men walk toward the dead corpse of John Vagis. Bernstein pushes the curtain back, gazes down, and pats the cadaver's torso, harshly! "The son of a bitch is dead. Finally!"

IRS agent Bill Henderson replies, "Thank God, indeed. I've been tracking this piece of shit for months, trying to pin his egregious crimes on him. But like Bernie Madoff, this prick made-off with billions, ruining countless people's lives, devouring their investments, and stealing their precious nest eggs. He's Wall Street scum!"

Dr. Bernstein nods. "Yes. I'm just glad I was able to help."

Henderson gazes at the dead corpse then up at the doctor. "I'm sure one day, after we're long gone and this information leaks out, they'll be many people who will praise your actions. But I gotta ask, do you ever feel remorse for playing God?"

Bernstein shakes his head resolutely. "Never. The only cases I take on in these circumstances are when I know for sure I'm doing the right thing. And ending John Vagis' deplorable reign of greed and corruption is not just righteous it's mandatory. Fortunately, that criminal driver started the ball rolling by sheer accident, but Vagis could have pulled through that accident if someone else here handled his case."

Henderson touches the cold cadaver and says, "But how in God's name did you manage to keep him in such a deep coma for so long?"

"Well, thank God for drugs, Bill. I infused some powerful toxins into his system. All legal ones of course, so it was a delicate balancing act. Furthermore, I took the liberty of manipulating his IntelliVue monitor to avoid reading his vitals properly, especially his surges in heart rate. Naturally, I couldn't have visitors seeing a healthy blip on the screen when they said or did something to encourage or revive him."

"But what about when his wife hugged him. Couldn't she feel his heart begin to beat faster?"

Bernstein smiles. "No. At times I had him on 800 milligrams of Metoprolol to lower his heart rate. I actually thought that alone would kill the bastard, but he took it in stride. But I'll tell you this much, he fought like a bastard to live."

Henderson smirks. "Yeah, of course he did. He lived like a goddamn king; racing around with his Tesla Model S or his Lamborghini or flying on his private jet to go golfing in Scotland, skiing in Austria, diving in Australia, or just living the good life at any exotic location on earth. It turns my stomach to see shysters like this get away with living high on the hog when it's off of the backs of other people's hard-earned life savings." He turns and gazes at the corpse, then punches it, firmly, angrily! "And the prick stole plenty from my brother Joey, who alerted me to this piece of shit. Joey had scored big with a restaurant chain that he started from scratch, a single little joint that he built up to a respectable nationwide franchise. It consumed his life, working countless hours around the clock. Now it's all gone. He had to declare bankruptcy to pay his way out of debt. It's maddening!" Again, Henderson swivels and jabs the body with an elbow to the ribs.

Bernstein grasps Henderson's shoulder. "Okay, I think it's best that I get this body out of here, before you use it as a punching bag. I don't want the morticians to get suspicious."

As Bernstein begins to disconnect the IV, Henderson shakes his head. "I hate this son of a bitch, and certainly would have loved beating the daylights out of him when he was alive, but I still don't have the guts to do what you did. Don't get me wrong, he deserved it, and I truly appreciate what you did, as I'm sure countless others will one day, but—" again Henderson shakes his head. "I just don't know how you can *actually* do it. You know, play God."

Bernstein calmly continues his work as he glances back at Henderson. "Bill, my father suffered through hell and survived the Holocaust. The Nazis exterminated people simply out of ignorance and hatred. That insanity is what made me abandon my belief in God. No God could ever condone innocent men, women, and especially children being exterminated like lice, and then being shoved into ovens like refuse. And if there is a God who plays by those ruthless and illogical rules, then men like *me* must take the reins and do something about it. Not for personal reasons, but for the betterment of mankind. If God can smite innocent people, then I can smite evil wretches. And this vermin of a man was an odious parasite that was a plague upon humanity, and that demanded extermination. It's that simple."

"Simple!?" Henderson exclaims. "But who gets to make those *simple* decisions? Sure, you feel you're a hundred percent correct in what you're doing, yet so too did the Nazis, not to mention how the Hutus slaughtered the Tutsis in Rwanda or how genocides occurred elsewhere. It's a recurring epidemic, as it seems everything in life is subjective. So where does this role of playing God end?"

Dr. Bernstein shrugs. "Well, as you believers say, 'Only God knows?' But as far as I, and many others, am concerned, justice has been served over the past six months. The suffering I put him through—where he could hear his loved ones cry and pine for him, yet was unable to do anything about it—has now finally ended with the legal authorization by his wife. The papers are all in order and John Vagis' rotten life and notorious racket are over."

Diligently, he disconnects the last monitor sensor from the corpse, and adds, "And God can now do whatever he wants with this *debris*. My job is done."

"Well, what if, like Lazarus, Jesus raises Vagis from the dead?"

Bernstein laughs. "You're talking to a man who was raised a Jew, one who never believed in Jesus anyhow. Moreover, Jesus is but only one divinity on this planet, and quite frankly, there haven't been any miraculous occurrences recorded since his crucifixion. So, why should I worry about what his or *any* god's wrathful intentions are for me? By their rules, I should have been smote long ago. So the odds against the Gods are in my favor." As Bernstein symbolically wipes his hands clean, he adds, "And get this, I did a little research; John Vagis was Lithuanian, and vagis in Lithuanian means *thief!*" As Henderson's eyes widen, Bernstein adds, "So by anyone's rules, it seems this termination was destined to happen after all. It was ordained. So just rejoice, an evil wretch has been eliminated from the world. John Vagis is dead!"

OBJECT LESSON

February 1947

It was a cold and brisk day on February 27, 1947, when Carmine Muscarelli entered the United States Naval Academy in Annapolis, Maryland. It was the proudest day in his fifteen-year-old life, at least up to that point. How he got to be appointed at that young age was a story in itself.

A month earlier, New York Congressman Jacob Javits had been walking the streets of New York with Mayor Fiorello La Guardia when the mayor struck up a conversation in Italian with Carmine's father, Salvatore, a humble street-cart salesman who couldn't speak English. The mayor translated Salvatore's words, which were soon directed at the congressman, being that Salvatore had an ulterior motive. Javits instantly bonded with the earthy man due to his similar humble roots, being that Jacob's mother had also been a street cart peddler, and Jacob recalled fondly how he helped his hardworking mother as a child.

Salvatore, however, cleverly switched topics and insisted that the congressman should meet his ambitious and studious son, Giuseppe, who had aspirations of going to the Naval Academy. Salvatore summoned his son, who obediently closed his science book and immediately ran over from across the street. Hence, it didn't take long for Javits to realize that Giuseppe indeed had the qualifications. The only problem was that Giuseppe was just fifteen, too young. That's when Giuseppe informed Jacob that his dear friend Carmine Muscarelli had recently died, and he wished to honor his memory by using his credentials, being that Carmine had been three years older. The congressman flatly refused, but Giuseppe happened to be as persuasive as his father, hence Javits eventually conceded and pushed the new enrollee's falsified papers through, and that's when Giuseppe Borelli officially became Carmine Muscarelli.

Carmine was all aglow upon entering the prestigious academy, as the young Bronx stallion had only known the scrappy kids in his impoverished neighborhood. Yet now he came in contact with young men from all parts of the country, many coming from wealthy families. As to be expected, most plebes and even midshipmen were white, in fact, at that moment, in 1947, only five African-Americans had gained admission, one of those being Leon Johnson. It didn't take long for Carmine to see that many of his fellow peers shunned or degraded Leon behind his back, despite the academy's fundamental practice of demanding moral integrity and their strict adherence to the Honor Concept, which is refusing to lie, cheat or steal.

As Carmine observed their bigoted actions and two-faced lies, he paused to reflect on the lie that changed his name and gained him access into the Academy. While he had moments of regret, Carmine recalled what he had said to sway Javits' mind, namely he reminded the congressman that the noble end justified the nominally underhanded means. Javits had balked at his suggestion, yet Carmine explained that Machiavelli's method didn't have to mean being brutally corrupt, such as killing or oppressing others to achieve an end. Carmine impressed upon Javits his unflinching confidence that his service to his country would yield great ends that would justify the means, ends that the congressman would one day be proud of.

But as Carmine gazed at all his fellow plebes, the feeling of camaraderie he had hoped to acquire didn't seem to fully materialize. As three and a half years passed—where he ascended from a plebe to midshipman first class—he engaged himself in excelling at a myriad of extracurricular activities, such as fencing, where, as captain, he led the fencing team to win the NCAA national championship in 1950. More importantly, he had managed to acquire his pilot's license, and here too rose to the top of his class.

However, in December of 1950, life was about to change, and not just for Carmine, as the Korean War, which had started five months earlier, had escalated to a point that now required the Naval Air force to assist. Over ninety Naval pilots volunteered, yet the final decisions were not theirs to make.

As they lined up for the final selections, Carmine stood proudly erect and ready. Strolling into the auditorium was Commander Averill Hilton, whose eagle vision cascaded down the line to scan the prospective pilots. Hilton was well acquainted with inspecting young men in their pristine uniforms, yet as he did, his head jolted! The glaring white lineup was marred by a black spot. His reaction was so plainly telegraphed that several naval pilots strained to hold back laughter, while others frowned, appalled. Nevertheless, Leon Johnson also caught the blaring twitch as he nervously swallowed a lump of humiliation while sweat began to ooze from his clean-shaven scalp.

Leon Johnson was born in Alabama and had suffered a long, hard string of insults and racial injustices that robbed him of a normal childhood. He suffered the indignity of sitting at the back of the bus, not being allowed to enter certain establishments, or even having to use public restrooms designated 'For Blacks Only.'

Yet Leon was a diehard Baptist who had expectations of following in his beloved Reverend's footsteps, who happened to be his father, as well as the father to two of Leon's half-brothers and his half-sister. But forgiveness was the Word of the Lord, so Leon and his community could not help but obey the divine wisdom of their Savior, even if that wisdom often contradicted itself, as the Seventh Commandment clearly stated otherwise. *But who are we mere mortals to question God?* Leon often thought. He would dedicate his life to being the Good Samaritan who would help his fellow brothers and sisters, no matter what color or how repugnant and offensive they might be, as all mortals must face the day of reckoning in the end. And Leon knew deep in his heart that Saint Peter would be waiting with open arms to embrace his obedient child of God, and would even swing open the golden gates and personally escort Leon up into the misty realms of ether and utter bliss.

But as Leon observed his superior officer's blatant look of contempt, his spiritual rock of confidence once again started to chip and crumble. He had suffered more indignities during his past four years at the Academy, as fellow midshipmen played cruel pranks on him or openly disparaged him, and now, in a moment of morbid piety, he even welcomed flying over Korea to be killed in action so he might rise up even higher into the heavens to return home to his dear father, *the* ultimate Father, who art in Heaven.

Leon closed his eyes, and in that moment prayed for deliverance. But when he opened his eyes, he recoiled!

Commander Hilton stood right before him, his piercing blue eyes like lasers that bore holes right into the retinas of Leon's shocked orbs. "What the hell are you doing, boy!? Napping?" Hilton barked.

Leon's nerves took hold of his tongue as he stammered, "N-no, S-sir! I was m-merely contemplating the great honor of b-being here, Sir, hoping to serve our gr-reat nation."

Leon's quick rebound impressed the commander, who cracked a smile. Or at least he thought he did, as his steely exterior didn't flinch an inch. "Well, then, I'm glad to hear it, son. What's your name?"

"Leon, Sir. Leon Johnson."

"I won't forget it," Hilton said in his deep, raspy voice. He then turned and marched to the center of the auditorium and faced the lineup. "As you all know, our great nation has become entangled in an Asian war that now requires our expertise, gentlemen. You are the cream of the crop, and I have high expectations of a clear and successful victory. But preliminary maneuvers are always a prerequisite to battle, and in that light, I will now assign flying partners." He glanced down at the clipboard in his hand, then scribbled out a few lines with his pen. He looked back up and said, "As in war, there will always be last minute changes, so best you all get used to it. The first two teammates will have a very special mission. And those two will be Carmine Muscarelli and Leon Johnson."

As several pilots stifled a snicker and others elbowed their buddies in relief, the commander summoned Carmine to the front. Carmine and Leon marched proudly up to the commander, clicked their heels and saluted.

The commander studied Carmine's face as he said, "I have chosen only two pilots to fly this recon mission before we engage in bombing sequences. You and Leon Johnson have been chosen for this most dangerous mission, as you will not have the full force of a squadron to protect you. You will lead this expedition, Muscarelli, being top in your class. Are you ready for such an undertaking, son?"

"Most definitely, Sir!" Carmine replied.

"As you know, such missions demand eagle eyes, so your vision will need to be tested once again."

Carmine's face twitched as his proud shoulders slightly wilted. "But, Sir. I must confess, as we are sworn not to lie. I am colorblind."

The commander squinted, perplexed, as did almost everyone in attendance. "How is that possible!?" the commander barked.

"Well, it's only two colors that I can't distinguish, Sir. If that's a consolation."

"No it is not!" Hilton retorted. "I don't know how this slipped through the cracks, Muscarelli, but I intend to find out!" He paused a moment, then added, "And just what might those two colors be?"

"Black and white, Sir."

The commander squinted once again, even more perplexed. "How can that be? Everyone can distinguish between black and white, son."

Carmine glanced unashamedly at Leon, then back at the commander. "Well *I* can't, Sir. To me they're both the same. So I'm delighted to fly this mission."

As Leon smiled, the commander's lips twisted with contempt as he seethed. "I don't find your little display of racial justice amusing, son!"

However, many pilots *did*, while a few others sighed with relief, glad that the cocky aviator was stuck with the Alabama blackie to fly a deadly mission.

The commander huffed and said, "Then I guess my last-minute decision to pair you two misfits together was sound." He gazed at both Leon and Carmine and added, "Report for your damn eye tests, pilots, and..." begrudgingly he added, "Godspeed!"

Two hours later, having passed their eye examinations, Leon and Carmine geared up and walked toward their two Corsairs.

Carmine patted the plane's metal belly and smirked. "You have to love it, they're sending us on a reconnaissance mission deep into North Korea with these leftover World War Two prop jobs."

Leon shrugged his shoulders. "I heard these babies did a swell job, though, Carmine." As he slipped on his gloves, he added in his Southern drawl, "Any hows, I hope to go in, get our intel, then get the hell outta there!"

Carmine nodded. "Yeah, but we'd be able to do that a helluva lot quicker if we had those new twin-jet-engine Banshees. I hear they go over five hundred and fifty miles an hour."

Leon worriedly shook his head. "Well, I'm more fretful about this doggone war. It's been like a ping-pong match; back and forth, win, lose, win, lose. Worse yet, now we got the Chinese joinin' the enemy. And those ratfinks sabotaged our 'Home Before Christmas' offensive. They're doggone traitors they are."

"Yeah, just like the Soviets," Carmine responded. "It

seems alliances mean nothing these days. No honor, no loyalty. But if the Chinks wanna stick their noses into our war, then we best get some good recon today, Leon, so we can pummel their yellow asses."

Just then Lieutenant Hildebrandt walked over and patted Leon and Carmine on their backs. "We're counting on you boys. I'm sorry we can't escort you all the way in, but we'll be in our chopper some thirty miles away, if you need us."

Leon cracked a nervous smile. "I wish it were thirty feet away, but I guess thirty miles will have to do."

Carmine slapped Leon on the back. "Don't worry, brother, I got your back."

Leon gave Carmine a quasi smile and a nod, but deep down believing otherwise; he didn't have any *brothers* in the Navy. Well, except for maybe his four fellow Negro officers from the Academy. But even at that, he was at loggerheads with Earl, who being a cynical realist from Detroit didn't like Leon's Southern, blind Baptist ways. Leon shook the thoughts away as he placed his helmet on his head and climbed into his blue Corsair. As he strapped himself in, he was overcome by a strange feeling—his fear and burdens, quite oddly, dissipated. His mind became unclouded. He was here to do a mission for his country, even if that mission seemed unclear, since North Korea wasn't threatening or invading the United States. But the new threat of communism was starting to make clear that Americans had to stand up to Stalin and Mao, who were indeed expanding their tyrannical influence.

As Carmine also readied himself, they each closed their canopies and nodded. Before long the two were up in the clouds and heading north over the 38th parallel and into enemy territory. They soon passed over a charred village with burnt-out huts from a previous raid and snapped a few photos with their specially mounted high-resolution cameras. Farther along they flew over muddy rivers and streams surrounded by thick woods. Then, unexpectedly, they whizzed past a small clearing. Unable to see exactly what it was, Leon circled around. Yet as he did, surface-to-air fire broke out into a hell-storm of lead that clipped his wing. Leon's Corsair pitched and began to nose-dive.

Carmine's eyes bulged as he gazed at Leon going down, then quickly swerved to avoid being hit. As fiery bursts of fire and black smoke billowed around him, Carmine hit the throttle and took off, while Leon glanced nervously upward, desperately seeking to locate where his brother was. But all he saw was the tail of Carmine's Corsair, which quickly disappeared into the clouds. Leon sniggered, half in humiliation and half in expectation, as he irritably drew his attention to the catastrophe at hand. He pulled back hard on the control wheel and tried to steady the ailerons as he swooped in low, just above the treetops. However, he couldn't keep the plane aloft, as the prop violently chewed up leaves and branches of the tallest trees, causing the blades and shaft to bend and the engine to explode! The plane careened into a thick set of bushes and came to a dead stop. Leon's head banged hard into the wheel, splitting open his forehead and cutting his lips, as rivulets of blood streamed down his face and onto his lap.

Half dazed, and in shock, he tried to reach down to unclip his harness, but it was bent and jammed tight. He summoned the will to survive and pulled hard. Yet still, nothing. He poignantly recalled his earlier, stupid notion of welcoming death in battle, and angrily slapped his helmet. "You damn fool!" He gazed up into the heavens, knowing not to expect seeing Carmine, but looking up toward his only Savior, and cried out, "Dear God! Help me, please! I don't wanna die! *Please!*"

Tears streamed out of his bloodshot eyes, which now lowered, only to see a terrifying sight! A team of twenty North Korean soldiers were heading his way in the distance, and closing in fast. He knew he had only seconds to possibly break free and run into the woods. Again, he pulled hard at the harness, but again, nothing! It wouldn't budge. His frantic eyes gazed up again to see the armed squad of soldiers bearing down on him, running faster and faster with each deadly step.

Leon's heart was racing, when, out of the clouds appeared a blue Navy Corsair with guns blazing! As Carmine swooped down low, he peered through the canopy—his eyes connecting with Leon's—and gave a thumbs up! As he whizzed past, Leon smiled, then gazed back down at the advancing soldiers. Only six were left!

Leon's heart lifted with joy, an intense and emotional elation that he had never experienced before. He clenched his fist and yelled, "Yeah! Mow those mothers down, brother!" With watery eyes he watched Carmine swoop in again for another kill. With a barrage of bullets, the last six soldiers were cut down, falling dead within yards of Leon's burning plane.

Again Leon struggled to unlock the harness, but to no avail. Yet a brief moment or two later, he saw the glorious image of Carmine running his way! As black plumes of smoke wafted through the air, Leon's vision was obscured. Yet piercing through the thick, black blanket of death was Carmine's fantastic face. "I told you I had your back!"

Leon couldn't hold back any longer and finally cried as he grinned. "I love you, brother!" With a choke and a whimper, he added, "I'm s-so glad to s-see you."

"And me you. Now let's get you out of here!" Carmine pulled a bowie knife out of his scabbard and cut through the thick harness. He reached in and grasped Leon under his arms and lifted him out, as they wobbled and stumbled to the ground. They looked at each other and began laughing. But a menacing rumble of gunshots ended their levity, as they got up and ran feverishly toward Carmine's Corsair. Yet as they approached, Leon's eyes widened! How could he forget? his frantic mind thought. Corsairs are single-seated airplanes! "Dear God, Carmine! What are we gonna do?"

Carmine grasped Leon and heaved him up. "Get your ass in there, and get going!"

Leon struggled to free himself. "Are you nuts!? I ain't gonna leave *you* behind!"

"Just shut up! We don't have time to waste. They'll be more NKs heading this way any minute." As he manhandled Leon's bloodied body into the cockpit, he added, "Besides, I radioed Lieutenant Hildebrandt. He's on his way with a chopper. He should be here any minute."

Carmine slammed the canopy shut, and yelled, *"Now get going!"*

Leon hesitated, but as blood oozed down over his eyelids, he wiped them clean with his sleeve and started up the engine. The immense joy he had recently felt by Carmine's arrival was now upended, as a gut-wrenching feeling of doubt and remorse gnawed at his heart and soul. Leon's hands and legs trembled as tears of regret marred his brown cheeks. With a deep breath and gritted teeth, Leon taxied out into the meadow and took off. Once aloft, he looked back to offer his brother a mournful wave, as he ascended into the clouds.

Carmine stood for an odd moment gazing up at his dear comrade as he finally disappeared. But the moment was broken when he heard a rustling of leaves some fifty yards away! He turned, only to see a group of North Koreans charging his way. He dashed into the woods, weaving his way into the unknown, as shots rang out and bullets whizzed over his head, some shredding the leaves into frightening bits of confetti. As he sprinted, the sounds of branches snapping, both under his feet and those being blown apart by gunfire, made his heart race faster and faster as he made his way into a clearing. By a miraculous stroke of fate, he heard the whooshing sound of a helicopter's blades. He gazed up to see a wonderful sight!

Lieutenant Hildebrandt was standing in the cargo doorway, waving for Carmine to run over, as the chopper lowered to within two feet off the grassy meadow. Hildebrandt bellowed, "Hustle it up, Muscarelli! They're on your tail!"

Carmine made a mad dash toward the chopper as he could hear the bullets buzzing by his head. The powerful surge of air from the chopper's blades pushed him back as he struggled to make his way to the open bay door. Just as he grabbed the railing, however, a bullet pierced through his lower back, blowing a hole out of his belly, which splattered blood and tissue on Hildebrandt's arm.

The lieutenant reached over and dragged Carmine in, then waved to the pilot, who pushed the throttle! As the chopper lifted, bullets pinged off its green metal skin, with one hitting and denting the tail blade. Within minutes, however, the helicopter maneuvered south and returned to base.

With radiant smiles of affection, Leon and Carmine embraced each other and laughed as they were escorted into the Mobile Army Surgical Hospital, where their wounds were surgically mended. They spent several weeks convalescing and being barraged by well-wishers and new buddies, as their brotherhood of two miraculously expanded from that moment forward, well into the future.

February 2017 Hofstra University - Sociology Class

I stood up and said, "And that aviators' tale concludes the first part of my lesson, class."

"You tell great stories, Mr. Rosetti. You're the best!" Jonathan O'Reilly called out.

I smiled and said, "Thank you, Jonathan, but sweet-talking me won't get you an A!"

The class burst out laughing, not because Jonathan was a poor student, but because they all knew he was a charmer, a clever manipulator who could sweet-talk the pants off a pauper.

I waved my hand for the class to simmer down, then continued, "As you all know, my stories are meant to entertain, but more importantly, to instruct. So I'd like all of you to seriously dissect this tale. Dig deep and analyze it to uncover its full import."

Nicole Sanchez raised her hand, and without waiting, said, "Well, since it's Black History Month, I think it was pretty clear, Mr. Rosetti, it was about how blacks were mistreated in the past." As four of the seven black students shot Nicole an evil stare, Nicole quickly defended her stance. "I know there's still racism today, but racism has existed since the beginning of time and has affected most races at one time or another. And let's face it; racism was far more prevalent back then. We've made tremendous progress."

"Oh, really? Have we?" Latasha Simpson retorted. "I still can sense what some white dudes are thinking by the way they look at me, and it ain't 'Hey honey, why don't we hit the clubs together and hang out, all brother and sister-like.'"

Jonathan O'Reilly, with his white freckled-face and red hair, leaned forward, gazed at Latasha, and said with a romantic smile, "Hey honey, why don't we hit the clubs together and hang out, all brother and sister-like?"

The class erupted with laughter, as Latasha smirked and rolled her eyes.

I interjected, "All right, calm down everyone! Yes, Jonathan brought levity to a serious situation, but sometimes laughter can heal wounds and hopefully bring people together, *if* it's done without sarcasm."

"Oh, it was, Mr. Rosetti, it was!" Jonathan quickly responded, as he gazed at Latasha's womanly curves, then at her irritated face. "I was dead serious."

"And if my brutha found out," Latasha said, "you would be *dead! I'm serious!*"

Once again the class erupted with laughter, as I waved my hands. "Enough! We're getting way off track here." I gazed at Jonathan. "You can make your romantic overtures in private," then looking at Latasha, I added, "And you and your brother can deal with him as you see fit." I looked at the class. "Now, getting back to this tale about navy aviators, what else about these main characters can anyone tell me?"

Jason Friedman blurted, "It's about bravery, Mr. Rosetti. It's how Carmine not only saved Leon's life, but how he also stuck up for him back at the academy."

Danny Chang chimed in, as he spoke to the class in general, "I'd like to know why racism was the first thing mentioned rather than heroics and good deeds? This isn't a Black History class, it's Sociology, about *all* humans."

"That's a salient point, Danny," I said. "Anyone have an answer for Mr. Chang?"

Brianna Westerman spoke out, "I think it's because we live in a society that focuses on negative things. Most of the news is about racism, killings, and corruption. And that racist viewpoint gets embedded into many people's minds."

"Another good point, Brianna," I said. "And it's not just the news, but also all forms of entertainment, as well."

"Yeah!" Jamal Brown cut in. "Like the killa lyrics in some songs."

"Or like a lot of the crap Hollywood pumps out!" Billy Harrington added.

"Yes," I said. "Many people unknowingly get manipulated by our manmade environment, which unfortunately can be as toxic as raw sewage. It plays a vital role in inculcating the masses. That's actually why I chose to teach sociology, as I feel compelled to enlighten you all to the unseen or overlooked aspects of life that do have a critical effect on us all. Which brings me back to my aviators' tale. Because you all pointed out the overt elements of the story, but missed the unseen aspects that beg to be revealed and analyzed."

As my eyes scanned the room, all I saw was a sea of puzzled faces. "Come on! As my teachers used to say, 'Put on your thinking caps!' What other observations can anyone else cite?"

The room remained silent for an odd moment, or two, until Jonathan raised his hand and said, "I would like to know more about Carmine Muscarelli. I mean, what made him so different than many of his peers?"

Billy added, "Yeah, what made him so brave?"

Jonathan looked at Billy. "I'm not just talking about brave. I also mean good-natured. I loved his *colorblind* line. In fact, I think I'll pilfer it."

As several students laughed, Latasha interjected, "Yeah, Mr. Charmer, you can try sweet-talkin' some poor sucka with that line. But it ain't gonna work on me!"

As Jonathan squinted, not appreciating the dig, I stepped in. "All right, keep it civil." I gazed at Jonathan. "But you've raised important questions. Now we're getting somewhere." As I looked out over the entire class, I added, "The basic question raised was: What in Carmine Muscarelli's past made him the way he was? Being both, brave, to sacrifice his life for a comrade, and colorblind, in regards to not seeing the difference between blacks and whites, as Carmine so eloquently stated."

Jonathan smirked. "But you never told us much about Carmine's past, only about Leon's, Mr. Rosetti. You hid that from us."

I smiled. "Yes, I did, and on purpose. I'm a sly dog, aren't I?"

As the class chuckled, I continued, "It was to make you all *think*, think beyond the active veneer of a story, or the selective events newscasters wish you to hear, or the TV shows or Hollywood movies that producers and directors with agendas wish to impart, and to ask, 'What is beneath the veneer?' What underlying story is there that is not being told, for to delve into the essence of any situation often yields another story, another truth, perhaps. Sometimes quite different than one would imagine."

I could see that some of my students' faces were still blank slates, but luckily, most appeared to be brimming with cranial activity, as their synapses sparked, eyes shifted in their sockets, and they wriggled themselves to sit up straight.

"So, yes," I said, "I left out an integral part of this story, the background of Carmine Muscarelli. At this point, I also must make a confession. That story happened to be true, and Carmine won a Medal of Honor. The only thing I changed, however, was Carmine's real name. It wasn't Giuseppe Borelli, it was Giuseppe Rosetti."

As all my students' eyes lit up, Nicole said, "Rosetti!? Was Giuseppe your father?"

"Yes, he was, Nicole. Or rather, he *is* my father. He is eighty-five years old now."

"Your father is a hero!" a student called out.

"And a good-hearted soul!" another exclaimed.

As others echoed similar praise, I said, "Thank you, yes, there is indeed an uplifting aspect to this story, namely how my father rose above the ignorance to judge Leon as a man. For as my father told me, 'A man's character is judged not by the color of their skin, but by their actions.' However..."

As students resumed a volley of praise, I interjected, "Hold on! Please. I appreciate your kind words, but I told this story not solely to honor my father, but to show you several underlying realities that can change your perspective and hopefully make you more fair-minded and positive in your way of thinking."

I walked to where my padded stool was and sat down, facing the class. "So the basic question is: 'What was my father's childhood like?' Well, I can say this much, it wasn't pretty." As many students' faces morphed from attentive smiles to penetrating stares of curiosity, I continued, "I imagine many of you expected him to have a happy childhood that groomed him to be a man of moral integrity and good character. Well. No, not really. He was never a choirboy or even attended Mass very often for that matter. But the truth is, people who come from hard backgrounds usually have two roads they can choose: the easy road of anger, hate, vengeance, envy and entitlement, or the rough road of hard work, which also requires a person to have hard skin, to not flinch when adversity strikes and to stay the course and seek the truth, which underlies the sea of flotsam that pollutes the surface. Sometimes it pays to dive deep, and swim under the waves of debris, to make it to the glorious port you seek."

The classroom was stimulatingly quiet—one of those rare moments when everyone was mentally in-sync, on the same wavelength, as if we were all breathing in unison, with our heartbeats pumping in rhythm, like an orchestra, featuring a variety of different instruments, yet all playing the same symphony.

"My father was born in the Bronx," I began. "However, *his* father had left Italy as an orphan at the age of sixteen. He came to America in the early nineteen hundreds all by himself, not speaking a word of English. But in his heart knowing that America would somehow offer him a better chance in life. He was partly wrong. The streets were *not* paved with gold, as so many erroneously thought. To survive, he became a street cleaner, shoveling horse manure on cobble-stoned streets, which were certainly not made of gold. He then sold hotdogs and corn on the cob. Basically, he did anything to make a buck." I raised my finger. "Hold on! Not *anything*. Let me clarify. Anything honest and legitimate that is. And my grandfather loved his wife and committed himself wholly to his family. These grounding principles were the bedrock of my father's life. As with any great person or entity, a good, strong foundation is critical."

Jonathan couldn't restrain his curiosity any longer. "But you said your father's childhood wasn't pretty.

Evidently he had a good father and a loving family. So what was the problem? It didn't seem so tough to me."

I smiled. "I'm getting to that, Jonathan. You see, even those who had a horrible father or mother or no parents at all, like my grandfather, don't live in a vacuum. Like osmosis, we all take in and take on traits from those around us, or from the things we read or see or hear. It's how we assess that influx of data that is most critical. However, while my father's home life was a raft of stability, he was soon thrust into the sea of Americans who spoke a different language and had been well groomed to look down upon immigrants, especially those like my father. Basically, Italians, in general, were derided as grease monkeys, Degos, Guidos, guineas, whops et cetera. In fact, there are more slur words for Italians than there are for Negros. Yet ironically the 'N' word is the only slur that can't be used. The unfortunate fact was that Al Capone, Lucky Luciano and the racketeers who established La Cosa Nostra or the Mafia, had also helped to establish the flotsam that spoiled the waters of the Italian community, which persists to this very day. Iconic movies, like *The Godfather, Goodfellas, Casino, The Untouchables* and *A Bronx Tail*, have kept the stereotype front and center."

Latasha interjected, "Mr. Rosetti, there are plenty of movies that portray blacks as thugs."

Nicole added, "Yes, so are you saying free speech, or the freedom to express ideas, is bad? That's a basic American principle and human right."

As several students got fidgety, I waved my hand. "No, no, that's not it at all. I enjoy those movies, just like the next person, and have no objections that they made movies that portrayed a sordid past. But there are several things that do concern me. There are countless mafia movies, even dating back to the days of Edward G. Robinson in *Little*

Caesar, yet how many Italian good-guy movies are there? Very few. There was *Serpico*, and, well, old TV shows like *Columbo* and *Petrocelli*, but that's all I can recall. And even at that, Columbo was not portrayed as an upscale polished person. He was a disheveled ragamuffin that drove a bomb of an old car. There's a serious imbalance. Furthermore, it has only been in recent years that the full story about America's mobsters is being investigated and revealed, as we now know that there were Irish and Jewish mafias, among others, that are finally rounding out the true picture, like *The Departed* or *Once upon a time in America*. Moreover, while everyone knows *The Godfather*, few, if any, know the other side of the Italian mobster story."

Jonathan smirked. "Okay, Mr. Rosetti, you egged us on enough. What's the other side to the Mafia story?"

"That should be clear enough," I said as I gazed at the class. "Any guesses?"

Jason Friedman blurted, "Yes, Elliot Ness! The FBI. The Untouchables."

"Very good, Jason," I said. "But..."

Jonathan shook his head, annoyed, "Hey! That was easy. You made it sound like a trick question. So what do you mean few, if any of us, would know that? Elliot Ness and the FBI were no brainers!"

I chuckled. "It wasn't a trick question, Jonathan. Yes, I'm referring to the FBI, but not Elliot Ness, who was shoved into the sea of flotsam for all of us to see. To get to the *real* essence, you must dive deeper."

A bolt of thought jolted Jason, as he shouted, "I got it! We need to ask, 'Who *founded* the FBI?'"

"Bravo!" I said. "Any guesses?"

Latasha's lips twisted. "I'm guessing it must be an Italian, right?"

"Good guess, Latasha. But as I said, few, if any of

you, will guess who that man was. In fact, I'll bet *none* of you know who it was. And that's the unfortunate part of this story. Once again, the media focuses on the negative Italian criminals, but rarely do they pay homage to the great people who organized the operations to battle and annihilate evil. And in regards to the FBI, the brilliant man's name was Charles Bonaparte."

"Bonaparte!?" Jonathan queried. "Like Napoleon, the tyrant?"

Nicole shook her head. "No, Jonathan, Napoleon was French, *not* Italian." She rolled her eyes. "Duh!"

I couldn't restrain a chuckle. "Actually, they *were* related, Nicole. Charles was Napoleon's great-nephew. And what many people also don't know is that the Bonapartes' lineage emanated from Tuscany. The French ruler and his American relative *were* Italians."

"Holy crap!" Jonathan blurted. "That's wild. I guess you're right, who could have guessed?"

Billy Harrington squinted. "Yeah. That's totally weird all right. An Italian founded the FBI."

I smiled as I looked over the entire class. "And I have an easy way for you all to remember it. FBI means Founded By Italian."

As the class chuckled, I added, "But we've drifted off course a bit. Time to navigate back to Giuseppe Rosetti's whitewater raft ride through the rapids of his youth." As the students simmered down, I continued, "My father was sent off to school, and while most of you think that's a horrible ride in and of itself, picture yourself not speaking English and having teachers who, at that time, were permitted to do and say things that today would have them in court and some locked up in jail."

With the student's attention once again captured, I continued, "My father came from a loving family, but they were poor, and so the battle to eliminate bedbugs or lice, which caused typhus in some cases, was a tough proposition, as tenement houses had thin walls with cracks that gave access to all types of critters. So even if you fumigated your apartment, it didn't matter, you inherited your neighbors' creepy crawlers, and the potential for serious diseases."

As several students shivered and others mumbled, "Ew, gross!" I continued, "So my father often had lice in his hair. As such, his teachers would smack him in the head with a rolled-up newspaper, since they didn't want to touch the filthy guinea, and drag him into the corner, where he would sit the entire class wearing a dunce cap." As eyes widened, I added, "Yes, dunce caps existed, and were used. Along with wooden paddles, that would whack my father's behind, or even crack down on his fingers or on the back of his head, which even caused him to get stitches. They often ridiculed him in front of the class, using the derogatory slurs of dumb Dego, greasy guinea, and then shoved him in the corner to be publically humiliated and largely shunned. Therefore, even learning how to speak English was limited, most of which he learned from observation and his friends. This added to his appearance of being simple-minded."

As many students' faces filled solemnly with compassion, I continued, "As a child, to have adults, especially teachers, publically dehumanizing you is a horrible environment to walk away from unscathed. But rather than cave in to the brutality, racist hatred, and ignorance, Giuseppe decided to take that other road, the high road of hard work, determination, and tolerance that also demanded tough skin. Along the way, he lost two brothers and a sister, who had all died before reaching puberty." I paused a moment to collect myself, then continued, "In fact, my father watched his older brother, Joe, get beaten to death by racketeers, because Joe had foolishly borrowed money he couldn't pay back." I gazed broadly over the class as my words became more poignant with each new sentence. "My father was only nine years old at the time. He was on his way home from school when he saw his brother being escorted into an alley. He ran to catch up to them, but stopped and slipped into a recessed doorway in the alley, petrified, as he watched six older thugs beat his brother to death with bats and broomsticks. It was a terrifying and humiliating experience, one that he swore he would never stand idly by to watch again. He studied hard on his own and eventually made his way into the Naval Academy. And that also explains why he would never let Leon Johnson sit trapped in his plane, knowing that North Korean soldiers would have tortured and beaten him to death, like the thugs who killed his brother."

The class sat speechless and visibly moved by the tragic tale, until Latasha said meekly, "That's a very sad story, Mr. Rosetti. Your poor father endured a lot of pain and abuse."

"Yes. He did," I replied, as I then looked at the class. "That's why it's imperative to open your minds. And the next time you hear a story, try to think of the unspoken elements that lie beneath the raging surface of deceptive flotsam. Only in that way can you get to the heart of the matter. Suffering is not exclusive to any one person or race. It comes in many forms and affects us all. But how a person or group addresses that suffering is also critical." As the clock struck the hour, the students uncharacteristically remained in their chairs, mesmerized, as I added, "Well, I see the hour is up. But I thank you, class, for your rapt attention and participation. Until tomorrow, this concludes my object lesson."

FBI: CHARLES BONAPARTE

For generations the Mafia thugs on the silver screen and their real-life counterparts have dominated the media and negatively typecast Italian-Americans, whereby coloring and distorting our perceptions.

Names like Capone, Gotti or Corleone have overshadowed those of Serpico, Giuliani or Freeh, who in the fields of law enforcement made noticeable differences in their respective departments. Whether it was Serpico uncovering the corruption within the police department, Giuliani significantly dismantling the Mafia and sleaze that plagued New York City, or Freeh serving as FBI director.

What's more, few Americans today realize that it was an Italian-American who founded what became known as the Federal Bureau of Investigation: the FBI. Charles Bonaparte, a man who served society throughout his life, created this establishment as a means to defend the nation and its values from criminals.

Charles Bonaparte's name may sound familiar, and rightly so. His grandfather, Jérôme Bonaparte, was in fact Napoleon Bonaparte's youngest brother. The Bonaparte family hailed from Corsica, which was originally an Italian island under the rule of the Republic of Genoa until it gained its independence in 1755. It was subsequently conquered in 1769 by French forces.

Meanwhile, on the other side of the Atlantic Ocean, Charles Bonaparte was born in Baltimore, Maryland in 1851. His parents were Jerome Bonaparte and Susan May Williams, whose father was one of the founders of the Baltimore and Ohio Railroad. Charles went on to graduate with degrees from Harvard College and Harvard Law School and became a successful attorney in his home state.

True to his upbringing, Bonaparte held a staunch belief in education as a way to cultivate one's expertise, which was grounded by a strong moral code. This combination drove him to prominence during an era mired in corruption and prejudices. At a time when Tammany Hall used brute force to bludgeon their enemies and robber barons went unchecked by legislation, Italian immigrants like Bonaparte were often harassed or shunned for their alien language and olive-colored skin. In 1891, one of the worst atrocities occurred when eleven Italian immigrants were brutally lynched in New Orleans. Added to the biases and abuses by laymen was that even the intelligentsia of the day were postulating pseudo-science to prove many races were inferior, including Italians, and were candidates for sterilization, as the ugly tenets of Social-Darwinism were taking root.

Nevertheless, Charles Bonaparte held true to his convictions of social justice and forged his way through the walls of corruption and prejudice to do what he believed was necessary. In 1881, he assisted in founding the National Civil Service Reform League. As the League's leader, Bonaparte spearheaded campaigns against racketeering not only in Maryland, but also on the national level. His multipronged attack was aimed at corruption among the electorate and the institutions of government. It was also aimed, quite uniquely, at the citizens, as Bonaparte believed the public needed to be educated about their responsibilities.

Bonaparte believed the United States—a nation governed by its citizens—could only be what its citizens were. If they were uneducated, unruly or uninterested, then no more could be expected of the government that represented them. In 1897, Bonaparte made a speech to this effect, saying: "To have a popular government we must, first of all, and before all else, have good citizens ... When we find any self-governing community afflicted with misgovernment, we can safely and fairly believe that it does not deserve a better fate."

That perspective eventually brought Bonaparte in contact with President Theodore Roosevelt. Both men were Progressives, and each advocated appointing experts in their respective fields in lieu of incompetent cronies who were often times selected by crooked politicians. Together, they formed a powerful duo.

President Roosevelt first appointed Bonaparte as Secretary of the Navy in 1905. He held that post for just one year until Roosevelt decided to place him at the head of the Department of Justice (DOJ) where his vast experience and proficiency with jurisprudence could flourish. It was here—as the 46th U.S. Attorney General—that Bonaparte utilized his knowledge, experience, and philosophy to combat the titans of industry in his day. While it was President Roosevelt who went down in history as the valiant trustbuster, Bonaparte was the fearless general in the shadows who was responsible for carrying out that onerous task.

Bonaparte waged antitrust battles against big businesses like Standard Oil, Union Pacific Railroad, and the American Tobacco Company. In doing so, he found that the information at his disposal was often times inadequate since the DOJ had no investigative unit. So he pressed to form his own elite staff. Having been forced to either hire private detectives or borrow investigators from other agencies, Bonaparte realized it was crucial to build a special team of operatives who were exclusive to the DOJ and trained either in covert fieldwork or as skilled examiners.

On July 26, 1908, Charles Bonaparte officially founded the Bureau of Investigation, ordering his new department, composed of 34 individuals (some of whom included veterans of the Secret Service), to report to Chief Examiner Stanley W. Finch, a position that would later become known as Director of the FBI.

Battling prejudice, industrial titans, crooked politicians and lawless citizens, Charles Bonaparte fought corruption until his term came to a close on March 4, 1909. Almost three decades later, his Bureau of Investigation would become what is today's Federal Bureau of Investigation. And while there exists a dark Mafioso stigma that plagues Italian Americans to this day, one of the world's most powerful investigative organizations—the FBI—was an agency founded by an Italian American.

(First published in *Italian American* magazine, October 2015.)

AUGUSTUS: *The Philosophy of Rule*

The life-giving gas rapidly expanded his tiny virgin lungs, following a brisk slap on the back. Thus was Gaius Octavius's first breath of life free from the womb. He would soon learn that it would be an endless struggle to maintain this precious gift, and that even though every breath one takes is by one's own effort, a supportive slap on the back is crucial to survival.

Now in his twilight years, the great ruler, who had come to be called Augustus, or most exalted as the name implies, was reflecting upon his long and illustrious career, with a concerned eye toward the future.

His early rise to power was marked by many near-death engagements on the battlefield, as well as in the perfidious political arena. Quite miraculously, those conflicts had been waged when he was only a mere teenager. Having outwitted perhaps the most learned sage of his age, Marcus Cicero, and beaten the most feared general, Marc Antony, Augustus—a solitary country boy who stepped out of obscurity to seize the greatest empire of his day—had shocked all.

With the lifelong aid of his most trusted general and loyal childhood friend, Agrippa, he had secured many years of peace, which he could now calmly reflect upon and cherish with a ripened grin. Priding himself on his earthy good sense, disdain for the ostentatious, and a paternal persona that would guide and elevate an entire empire, Augustus established what he believed was the only solution to a corrupt and war-ridden Rome. His decisions proved right: he presided over a renewed golden age for over four long decades and had made Rome the wonder of the world. Augustus had much to be proud of.

Inside his modest and unassuming residence, nestled on Palatine Hill, Augustus sat statuesque and pensive on a simple wooden bench wearing a plain toga, looking more like a plebeian than the *Princeps*. Several feet to his left, his wife Livia stood brushing her thick gray hair. She, too, was quiet, yet for a different reason.

The seventy-six-year-old ruler was ill and facing his last months on Earth, and the monumental quandary of choosing a successor weighed upon him heavily. With three bloodline heirs prematurely dead, Augustus had been forced to adopt Livia's austere son, Tiberius, from her former *matrimonium*. Meanwhile, Livia was a strong and manipulative mother who wanted very much to see her son take the reins. However, knowing that her husband was not one to be easily swayed, Livia remained tactfully calm as she went about her daily activities.

Augustus had been gazing at Livia out of the corner of his eye, when he lifted his head. "Livia, with the dreadful chain of misfortune that has besieged me, your beloved son is now well seated to acquire my title. But you must know that I still have serious reservations."

Livia turned and smiled diplomatically. "Augustus, my dear, I have seen you on your deathbed far too many times and you have always managed to miraculously defy the gods. Why do you think those stories of your divine birth spread so quickly? Romans know of no man stricken as often as you or as strong-willed and brilliant as you. You're a unique gift to Rome and your time of passing has not yet come. So, other options may still arise."

Augustus frowned. "I know good fortune has shone upon me many times in the past, Livia, but I've played this role well beyond anyone's expectations, especially my own, and the final act approaches." Augustus peered gravely at the two theater masks painted on the wall. Looking back at Livia, he continued, "My appointment by my great-uncle Julius was not made in haste or from lack of choice. My decision is likewise crucial. Believe me, I am pleased that Tiberius is a competent general, but I can never forget how he abandoned us, as well as the Senate, by fleeing to Rhodes. It was inexcusable. That I allowed his return speaks as much of my forgiveness as it does of my back being pinned against a wall. No leader should find himself ensnared in such a position. And so, I anxiously await the divine guidance of the Sun. Apollo must shed light on this final and most vital decision—he must!"

Livia turned slowly and gently picked up a golden talisman; it was a gift from Tiberius, who had received the reward for his massive triumph in Pannonia. With a loving smile, Livia proudly turned toward her pale husband. "You worry in vain, my dear. Sometimes you afford superstition too much muscle, whether relying upon a piece of sealskin for good luck or the great Apollo for guidance. I trust your good judgment and so should you; it has never failed you. Granted, you may have wanted Marcellus, Gaius, or Lucius to be your successor, but, as you know, unforeseen events are a part of life. Perhaps their tragic deaths were for a reason. You know I loved and raised Gaius and Lucius as my own sons, but you are far too wise not to have noticed their inexperience or ingratitude. Tiberius may have run away to Rhodes, but perhaps that was to allow his younger relatives unhindered access to your title."

Augustus' right brow pinched as he shook his head. "Livia, I do not need or expect Tiberius to think for *me!* I was grooming those boys, who came from the loins of my daughter and best friend, Agrippa. So whatever decisions I made, Tiberius should have simply obeyed. As it was, his foolish retreat has only shed doubt upon his own abilities and *mine* for choosing such a capricious young man."

Livia irritably slammed the talisman down. "Capricious!? You mean the young man who defeated countless armies that could have wreaked havoc all across Rome? Furthermore, that young man is now in his fifties! You were in your teens when *you* sought power."

Augustus grinned. "My dear, being a great general or simply great in years does not necessarily make a great politician. My great-uncle Julius and my feeble, former *triumvir* Lepidus are both proof of that."

Sensing the weight of his words and the sensitivity of the topic, Livia took a deep breath and calmly resumed brushing her hair. "That's true, however, Tiberius has shown great promise, and if chosen, I know he will honor your memory. You shall indeed be hailed as Rome's first and most glorious *imperator*."

Augustus frowned. "You know I dislike that title, Livia!"

"Oh, yes, how could I forget, *Princeps*, or first among equals, is your preferred title. But we both know our fellow Romans all hail you as *Augustus* Caesar. Your deification is assured, and rightly so."

Augustus shook his weary head. "You miss the point. Control and respect cannot be won by arrogantly dictating one's own divinity like the pharaohs. Yes, I deified my uncle Julius and that title has been bestowed upon me, but Romans know that title is just to signify greatness among mortals. We look up to and pray to the gods, Livia. The pharaohs truly believed they were gods and had tremendous pyramids built for themselves and their treasure. This mistake I know all too well. Look how Romans still adore the great Cincinnatus. When Rome was under siege, they beckoned him out of retirement and appointed him dictator to secure Rome from conquest. He left his plow and fought a winning campaign for the Republic, only to magnanimously decline leadership in its aftermath." As Augustus continued passionately, he clenched his fist, "He had Rome in the palm of his hand, and could have ruled like a god, but *no*, he gave Rome back to the people. I have always acted as a fellow citizen of Rome. Yes, *the first citizen*, but a citizen nonetheless. What remains most important, my dear Livia, is what's best for Rome!"

Livia's stiff posture softened slightly as she rubbed her forehead. Pivoting about, she purposefully walked toward him and placed a basket of fruit by his side. With a firm hand planted on her hip, Livia looked squarely into his eyes. "I don't see how that makes a difference. Ramses and many other great pharaohs ruled with iron fists, and the people labored hard and prayed to their greatness, didn't they?"

Nonchalantly, Augustus picked up a cluster of grapes and began freeing them from the vine. Noticing his great grandchildren in the next room, he began tossing the grapes into a nearby bowl, as he replied serenely, "Yes, control they had, Livia, but it was total enslavement, smoldering with resentment. Look what became of Egypt—their laws, language, and culture have all but completely vanished. We may work our plebeians almost as hard, but their minds very seldom abandon hope. Shackling an entire populace is suicide for the public and the state. That explains why the lure of Roman citizenship, legal rights, and a civic duty for religious ritual play such crucial roles in appeasing the masses. The reckless and decadent behavior that destroyed our Republic must always serve as a warning. Roman law must prevail, as excessive freedom promotes mischief and moral decay. Furthermore, it is imperative that we share this ideal of hope and prosperity with all our new provinces, regardless of their distance from Rome. This, my dear, is paramount."

With a clatter of little feet, three of their great grandchildren ran by, each grabbing a handful of loose grapes from the bowl. Merrily, they ran off to the sunny courtyard and began handing some of the grapes out to their begging friends. Augustus smiled, and then looked down at the remaining cluster of grapes in his hand.

He raised them up, and looked at Livia. "You see, my dear, these grapes are still shackled and are destined to my sole wants and whims. I can eat them for nourishment or even wastefully destroy them. However, those that I freed have traveled beyond the walls of this room and managed to nourish and benefit many others. Likewise, we Romans need to travel to other lands and spread this wealth and nourishment."

Livia smiled and nodded admiringly. "Yes, I see your point. But how much freedom did those grapes truly have? *You* freed the grapes and then purposely tossed them in the bowl. So, weren't *you* the silent orchestrator of their destiny?"

Augustus smiled. "Now you are finally seeing the beauty of using power wisely. The minds of the masses must be carefully and subtly conditioned. They must be able to believe that they are free and part of a greater whole, and that there is some ray of sunshine to brighten their days. Why do you think I engage Romans in many grand tasks? It's to remain productive for Rome, for themselves, and to prevent the grapes from rotting on the vine. However, unlike the pharaohs, I shall not humiliate them by demanding harsh labor to construct useless edifices for my own personal glory. Our glorious building projects may serve my personal agenda, but that agenda is for the benefit of Rome and its citizens. No other regime in history has bequeathed to the plebeians the public works we Romans have. Moreover, these great works shall rival and surpass all before us. And between the policies I've created and those of the Republic that I've left in place, Rome will prevail."

Livia turned, and as her eye caught the dark shadow of the sundial in the courtyard, she scoffed pessimistically, "Yes, but the almighty Sun over Egypt has long since set; it has abandoned Egypt's noble attempts at greatness and its people, as it will one day Rome."

Despite his crippling ill health, Augustus rose steadily to his feet and declared firmly, "Never! Providence has always watched over Rome. Even our great poet, Virgil, elucidated this fact." As Augustus continued passionately, his arms reached radiantly outward. "Our grand systems of roads are spreading over distant lands like a sprawling laurel tree, and as it continues to sprout healthy new branches, keep in mind, Livia, that Rome remains its royal root. What were once barbaric lands are now civilized provinces—learning and benefiting from our laws, customs, and grand feats of engineering. Egypt's glamorous eyes only saw Egypt, and blindly neglected the world around her. The grand pyramids may have been magnificent, they may have touched the sky, and they certainly consumed a nation's time and resources, but they only housed one small selfish and shriveling man, a man who callously neglected the needs of an entire nation so that he alone could be glorified."

As Livia stood mute like a lectured pupil, with eyes wide, Augustus pointed out the window at the majestic city, and continued, "My intention, Livia, has always been to bring the glories of Rome to the rest of the world, by building grand forums, temples, aqueducts, and markets wherever we traveled. Moreover, my creation of the *Vigiles Urbani* to apprehend criminals and fight fires in our cities has finally brought order and safety to the chaos that has plagued mankind since its very inception. Those gifts I bequeathed to all of our citizens, and it is the duty of all my successors to ensure the same for all future citizens of Rome. It is our destiny!" Taking a deep breath, Augustus expelled his last charge, "Therefore, Egypt's blind ambition is something I, as a Roman, never understood, could never embrace, and shall never forget! And if my successors fail to fulfill my vision, Livia, it is not because of any so-called cataracts I may have, but rather their own blindness. Therefore, I pray to the gods, my dear, that your son will not only have the bravado to repel foes, but also the brains to see clearly! Rome's future, nay, our civilization's very future, depends on it."

††††

Through instinct and observation, Augustus knew his new empire needed a new direction, as well as initiatives not employed by the Egyptians or any previous regime. Augustus was not what we today would call a well-groomed intellect, however, his innate common sense, extremely organized and analytical mind, along with the ability to learn from his and others' mistakes, made his efforts and achievements beyond brilliant. During Augustus' careful and precarious rise to ultimate power, he had wisely left the Senate and Republican infrastructure intact, albeit with some clever revisions. These policies all had clear objectives.

First, Augustus understood the deep political roots and social-economic pedigree of wealthy patricians. They had held and maintained their positions of power for many decades, with some senators like Brutus having family trees extending back 500 years to the founding of the Republic itself. As such, they and their entrenched network would not easily relinquish power. Caesar had arrogantly underestimated them and it proved fatal.

Henceforth, Augustus needed to purge the Senate of those who plotted against his adoptive father; those who remained needed to be cajoled and placated, which could not be achieved by arm-twisting or arrogantly stripping them of power. Furthermore, the Roman citizens of the day had had enough of civil strife. Over the previous two decades they had been dizzied by having to take sides with one potential usurper after another. Loyalties were strained and national enthusiasm drained. Therefore, it was prudent of Augustus to leave the Senate, and its web of influence, intact to some degree.

Second, Augustus understood that more than one

person with a handful of cohorts was needed to run a sprawling empire. The bureaucratic infrastructure that worked so well for the Republic would serve him well too, as long as he made continual subtle revisions that would wrest the ultimate and abused power from the aristocracy.

Third, and quite ingeniously, Augustus realized the importance of creating a new cultural identity for his government that he could share with all the Roman provinces. In an act of perceptive statesmanship and benevolence, Augustus bequeathed what was available in the illustrious capital city to the distant provinces. This extensive policy had many cultivating facets.

To Augustus, it meant that all newly acquired provinces would be outfitted with the utilitarian effectiveness and the grandness that Rome itself enjoyed—this would be an integral part of the glue binding a sprawling and diverse populace. Grand forums, public markets, housing with running water, public baths with spectacular saunas, and other cutting edge facilities not only improved the standard of living, but equally important, it elicited pride of community and Roman culture.

This psychologically effective technique was not lost on subsequent leaders, even those well beyond Rome, and would influence many European nations and America in the distant future. Not only did the American founding fathers emulate Roman architecture and city planning, but even today, the construction of shopping malls and familiar franchises sprawling across America is unifying the nation, visually and psychologically. There is a downside to this trend—namely, the decline of uniqueness—but the mission of spreading unity, national identity, and different forms of progress is achieved.

Needless to say, America's founding fathers

scrutinized and utilized many facets of Augustus' political, economic and engineering initiatives, thus validating the immense indebtedness Americans and most other Western nations today have for ancient Rome, and in particular for Augustus.

Moreover, the titanic skills required for achieving all those amazing goals, especially considering that Augustus' provincial education was cut short, thus necessitating a need to devour knowledge, as well as discern the virtues and treachery of human nature, whereby he could act decisively and judiciously, remain to this day immeasurably off the charts.

This new breed of leader, which as Suetonius proclaimed "held idealism over egotism in a noble effort to create the best possible government" had not only made a monumental beginning for Rome, but more importantly, one of seismic proportions for Western civilization. Augustus had only been a teenager when he began his grand and noble quest, yet he prevailed against tremendous odds, and created an amazing enterprise that would profoundly imprint itself upon all future generations. This young man, born Gaius Octavius, and later exalted as Augustus, has been justifiably called "The Father of Western Civilization."

MARCONI: *Radio & Wireless*

A frigid Canadian blizzard hammered the sides of the cast-iron locomotive as it chugged its way southward along the frozen tracks. Snowflakes melted rapidly as they slammed into the steam engine's coal-fired boiler tank, while the front-mounted apron plowed through the mounting snow.

Anxiously peering out one of the train's rear windows was Guglielmo Marconi, watching as his towering communications aerial disappeared under a blanket of driving snow.

Over the past several years, Marconi's notoriety for pioneering wireless transmissions had escalated the demand for his presence. Having just finalized the progress-check on his new broadcast antenna in Nova Scotia, Marconi was now heading south to Massachusetts.

Arriving in Cape Cod, on January of 1903, the beleaguered steam engine finally thumped to a screeching halt. As Marconi made his way to the exit door, he hunched over slightly to peer out the train's long series of windows.

Through a thin veil of steam, Guglielmo could see a line of officials standing among a crowd of spectators. Suddenly the doors slid open, and the conductor escorted Marconi off the train. Meanwhile, dignitaries flocked to greet and shake the celebrity's hand.

A porter brazenly edged his way to the fore. "Mr. Marconi, I have your baggage several cars back. Please, come this way."

As they traversed the platform, soft billows of white steam belched out from the sides of the massive locomotive. Marconi and the porter were soon enshrouded in vapor, inciting Guglielmo to cough. Meanwhile, black plumes of soot rose from the engine's grimy stack and dissipated into the frigid air. Unexpectedly, the train's deafening whistle blew, forcing Marconi and his escort to step out of time. As the train rolled forward, the crowd simultaneously split apart.

Walking toward them, with a valiant gait, was a stocky man with a mustache and round spectacles. Two men curiously flanked this audacious man, and as he approached, it became apparent that it was none other than America's twenty-sixth president, Theodore Roosevelt.

"Good day, Mr. Marconi! I trust your journey has been a safe one?" Roosevelt said, as he firmly grasped Marconi's hand and shook it vigorously.

"*Si...* I mean yes, Mr. President," Marconi replied in broken English.

"This is an historic day!" Roosevelt bellowed excitedly. "Your new device is beyond revolutionary, Mr. Marconi. It is startling! Yes, startling. And *that*, I relish wholeheartedly."

"Many thanks, Mr. President," Marconi said as the porter handed him his briefcase. Guglielmo slipped the porter a tip, then looked back at Roosevelt. "Many countries have also been quite interested as well. I have a most taxing schedule these days. But I'm glad to see that America is taking part in this grand effort by authorizing my antenna here at Cape Cod."

The President smiled, revealing his trademark set of teeth, as his two bodyguards subtly scanned the perimeter. "Yes, Mr. Marconi," Roosevelt replied, "We Americans love to push, or at least aid in pushing, the barriers of engineering and science. My efforts in Panama will soon prove to the world the grandest engineering feat of our time. But I must say that I was very impressed with your wireless coverage of our American Cup four years ago. I received word that many sailors thought your new device was extremely modern, and described it as 'not of this world.' I myself cannot fathom how on earth you can transmit messages through thin air, Mr. Marconi. Are you a magician, like that other new sensation, Harry Houdini?"

Marconi chuckled. "No, Mr. President. I assure you it is *not* magic, but rather pure science. Science *is* the future. As you may know, most of my work has been commissioned by England, as my patent in 1897 marked the premiere of my radio waves. Germany likewise has an immense interest in my wireless communications. However, since the Germans and I were unable to reach an agreement, Karl Braun founded their Telefunken Company." Marconi turned his collar up as the frigid wind howled and snow flurries danced across the air. "Luckily for me, Mr. President, the Germans lag far behind. But that is why today is very important. A few weeks ago, my system sent several messages from Canada to England. For that feat I have already received a congratulatory telegram from your illustrious inventor, Alexander Graham Bell. But, here today, America shall make *this* feat even more world renowned."

Roosevelt patted Marconi on the back heartily, then grasped Marconi's shoulders and swiveled him toward the huge antenna. Firmly wrapping his arm around the inventor, Roosevelt began to guide Marconi up the path. "Well, let's get the show on the road, my good fellow! There's nothing more exhilarating than breaking world records. Let's just hope this contraption of yours has the wherewithal to shoot my message across the Atlantic."

Now harnessed to, and trotting with, the energetic president, Marconi replied, "I have every bit of faith that it will, Mr. President. My wireless transmissions travel through the ether, but, as you know, the Earth is round. Therefore, after two hundred miles or so, the straight trajectory of light and sound waves leave the planet, shooting outward into space. Hence, the Houdini trick, as you say, was to find a solution, which I have indeed!"

Roosevelt gazed into Marconi's eyes. "You see, I knew you were a magician!"

Marconi laughed. "Well, perhaps you're right, Mr. President. After all, science *is* magical."

Slowing to a leisurely pace, the two great men uncoupled themselves and finally reached the radio control center. A throng of technicians and journalists cluttered the scene. With great anticipation, Marconi approached his newfangled device and made some minor adjustments. The inventor then turned and looked at Roosevelt with a sense of pride. "Mr. President, be my guest. British King Edward VII awaits your greeting!"

Roosevelt nodded and eagerly strode over to the communications board. Turning to make sure everyone present had a fair view of the historic moment, Roosevelt flashed his charismatic smile and looked back down at the apparatus. Cracking his knuckles, Roosevelt then placed his finger on the machine. With a silent dispatch, Roosevelt's greeting was sent off to the British king.

An eerie calm fell over the room, as everyone glanced at one another then back at the idle transmitter. Roosevelt stood silent, looking at the equally silent gadget. As he looked at the transmission panel intensely, ten seconds suddenly felt like ten minutes. His eyebrows pinched. The president now began to feel as though nothing actually occurred. As several dignitaries and journalists stood uneasily nearby, Roosevelt looked haplessly at their bewildered faces, then inquisitively at Marconi. The president felt utterly foolish. "Excuse me, Mr. Marconi, but I find it a tad odd not speaking to someone face to face. This seems most unnatural. When will..."

No sooner did Roosevelt say those last words, than the distant king's response rang out. Roosevelt spun about and looked excitedly down at the transmitter.

"By God, Mr. Houdini, your contraption works!"

As the crowd burst into laughter with a hardy round of applause, Roosevelt stepped over and firmly embraced Marconi. As the two men chuckled, Marconi discreetly turned his head to expel a sigh of relief.

Journalists busily jotted down their notes while photographers snapped photographs. Meanwhile, Roosevelt and Marconi congratulated the communications team, and then headed out the door to take a leisurely stroll along the cape.

Roosevelt was deeply moved. "Mr. Marconi, I must say that scientists fascinate me. They are very much like fortune-tellers. So, tell me, what do you foresee in the future for wireless?"

Marconi secured his hat, while a chilly breeze wafted across the shoreline. He then glanced at the expansive ocean, then back at Roosevelt. "Well, Mr. President, I see many uses for my device. But perhaps its first great use will be at sea. Although many nations are becoming more interested, they still haven't mandated its use in naval vessels."

Roosevelt looked over with a knowing glance. "Yes, I've been informed by my naval department that they declined to institute your wireless system. However, I was also informed that you have some serious issues with static. Is that true?"

Marconi stopped in his tracks, as Roosevelt followed suit. "Yes, Mr. President, there is one minor issue. But I have already worked out a solution. Unfortunately, I wasn't able to reveal that solution to your naval administrator, since I have yet to secure its patent. And believe me when I say that many inventors and nations are desperately seeking to unearth my newest secret developments. It's a dog-eat-dog world, Mr. President."

Roosevelt nodded. "Indeed it is. I know that more than most, Mr. Marconi. But, I'll have to stand by my navy's current position, that is, until you are able to confidently publicize your remedy."

Marconi's face mellowed. "That really is a shame, Mr. President. Do you realize that your navy still relies upon carrier pigeons to send communications?"

Roosevelt smirked then chuckled. "Yes, I suppose our system *is* for the birds!"

Marconi mildly smiled as he stoically continued, "But seriously, Mr. President, both Italian and British ships have already upgraded to wireless, its uses are not just strategic, but life preserving. Many ships have been lost or wrecked at sea, and only due to wireless distress-transmissions were they effectively rescued. Let's be honest, sailing the vast oceans, while severing contact with land, is surely a recipe for disaster."

Roosevelt nodded firmly as he grasped Marconi's arm and ushered him toward the cape. "Well, I can see your point, Mr. Marconi. I do believe you have something enormous here, and I trust that it will one day reshape world communications. So be assured, America *will* keep a close eye on your newest developments. That I guarantee!"

†††

As this semi-fictional vignette indicated, Marconi did erect his radio station in Canada, and did take a train down to Massachusetts. There, he met President Theodore Roosevelt, who made that historic transmission. As inferred, Marconi was in fact nervous on this occasion, for as he later confided to a journalist: "The mere memory of it makes me shudder. It may seem a simple story to the world, but to me it was a question of the life and death of my future." Marconi's future, however, was secure, as was his amazing wireless invention.

The world of travel in the early 1900s, before the advent of flight, was firmly dominated by the sea. Therefore, all ships leaving port were instantly rendered mute, leaving their fate to the unpredictability of carrier pigeons. Hardwired telegraph cable was an up-and-coming technology, but it left any movable land vehicle or sea vessel severed and perilously isolated. Eventually, Marconi's wish was realized when it became mandatory for all vessels to carry wireless. However, even open communications at sea had to be manned by fallible humans.

A few short years later, on April 15, 1912, the *SS Titanic* set sail on its maiden voyage. In the dead of night, amid the frigid North Atlantic seas, the colossal vessel struck an iceberg. The horrific disaster shook the world, as over 1,500 people died, drowning in the icy and desolate waters. Yet, it was solely due to the *Titanic's* wireless distress signals that 700 people survived. In a British report the next day, Marconi was rightfully praised for making that miracle possible. Oddly enough, Marconi was scheduled to travel aboard the *Titanic,* but at the last minute rebooked an earlier passage safely aboard the *SS Lusitania.* That ship, too, would later face its own disaster; hence, Marconi escaped death twice.

Marconi's wireless miracle had previously attracted the attention of many other nations. In February of 1904, Russia and Japan broke out into war. Each side purchased Marconi's apparatus. The Japanese equipped their entire naval fleet, while the Russians only outfitted their ground forces, foolishly sparing expenses with their navy. A mere three months later, the Japanese triumphantly defeated the Tsarist's in battle, which in turn ignited Russia's Bolshevik Revolution.

By 1909, the impact of Marconi's invention became universally clear, as he was awarded the Nobel Prize for Physics. However, by 1922, Marconi was already predicting further uses of his wireless technologies. He spoke of microwaves, which later developed into a broad array of modern uses, and described how waves, when transmitted and bounced off objects, could be calculated on their return. This became known as radar, and subsequently that concept engendered sonar. These two technologies had their first and most profound application in WW II.

Notwithstanding the brilliant leadership of FDR and Churchill, the most important factors in WW II were wireless communications, radar, cryptography, LCVP landing crafts, and aircraft technologies. The engineering feats of R.J. Mitchell's Spitfire, and his pre-war determination to advance his airplane during competition rivalries with German aviators, were likewise critical to England's early survival. Additionally, Marconi's wireless communications, and later radar, became England's most crucial defense mechanisms against Germany's blitzkrieg.

Many scientists had contributed to the early development of radio. Akin to other inventors who had borrowed ideas from their peers and predecessors to obtain a solution, Marconi was no different. Scientist/inventors, such as Nikola Tesla, Karl Braun, Heinrich Hertz and most importantly, David Hughes, who had actually made the first basic wireless transmission years earlier, all made preliminary and crucial developments. However, Marconi was the one who persisted in the venture, utilized new research, connected the dots, added his own genius, and made it functional on a broad and curved global scale. David Hughes, who, besides Tesla, had the most rights to lay claim to this technology, had even been interviewed regarding Marconi's world fame. Thus he stated, "His efforts at demonstration merit the success he has achieved."

And it's precisely because of Marconi's ability to demonstrate steady results that he secured the long-standing interest and venture capital of large British investors. Meanwhile, other scientists, like Hughes, failed to generate interest and gave up; while men like Tesla, who had a superior brilliance for invention, lost funding due to poor business management or simply being too distracted by other alluring endeavors. Hence, this explains why Marconi succeeded while other brilliant minds failed.

Additionally, this elucidates why Marconi's radio transmitting devices became prominent in England, rather than America. Fortunately, England had seized Marconi's inventive and industrious skills early on, for without the eventual development of wireless transmissions or radar, England would have suffered far greater losses during Hitler's blitzkriegs and naval assaults. Some analysts even suggest that England would have been annihilated.

Therefore, Marconi was crucial to England's effective use of radio and radar during WW II. Furthermore, this reveals why the Americans attempted to discredit Marconi, who had lived in Fascist Italy, by rallying behind the newly Americanized citizen and scientist, Nikola Tesla. This conflict erupted into the Marconi vs. Tesla case in 1943, which naturally resulted in the Americans overruling Marconi in favor of Tesla. Interestingly enough, the American government had awarded Marconi the patent for radio decades earlier, overlooking Tesla. Henceforth, the American government cunningly sided with the party whom they would not be required to pay royalties to in their own quest to control radio.

However, while Marconi admitted that his early progress had borrowed ideas from Karl Braun, Hertz, Tesla, and others, his success was a result of personal research, trial and error, inventiveness, and focused determination. This materialized into his successful transmissions across the sea between mainland Ireland (and Wales) to surrounding islands, thus leading to his development of stronger frequency waves, which led to his famous transatlantic transmission. Marconi was obsessed with finding the solution to make wireless waves travel even farther. Earth's curvature had many believing that longer wavelengths might be the solution, yet Marconi found the opposite to be true. His quest led to the correct answer, and thus the ability to send wireless waves around the world.

After World War II, the Cold War between the Soviet Union and the United States immediately ignited the Space Race. All space communications, including ground-control's wireless remote systems, which guided NASA's space vehicles, were all made possible by Marconi's wireless technology. Moreover, satellite communications, cell phones, GPS, Bluetooths, wireless Internet, microwaves, and various remote control systems all evolved from the one driving force that perfected and then brought wireless to the world market: Guglielmo Marconi.

Roosevelt & Churchill:
Saviors of Western Civilization

Blazing through the wind in his shiny blue Ford convertible, Franklin's polio-ridden body showed no sign of burden as he deftly manipulated the custom hand levers. Above all things, Franklin loved driving and swimming, as it was only during those times that his crippling paralysis, which robbed him of the use of his legs, seemed to vanish. Only then could Franklin regain the full vigor of his youth.

Dashing to Hackensack airport from his home in Hyde Park, New York, the president rapidly approached the crudely constructed airfield. It was June 19, 1942.

With the landed airplane now in sight, Franklin cut the wheel and fishtailed onto the airstrip's dirt runway. Excitedly, he squeezed the accelerator lever with his hand, as the Ford's whirling Firestones churned up huge billows of dust, forming a long amber wake. With his hair flapping in the breeze, Franklin rumbled up to the small Piper J-3 Cub and came to a sliding stop. As the dust cloud passed by his head and over the front hood, Franklin could see the plane's tiny passenger hatch fling open.

Franklin's fingertips impatiently tapped the steering wheel as he awaited his guest. The plane's air-cooled engine cut back to an idle and the small prop gradually whooshed to a stop. It was then that Franklin could vaguely see a stout figure slowly emerging from the fuselage's square-shaped threshold.

Impulsively, Franklin's arm shot upward and waved, as he yelled, "Winston, how good to see you again!"

The robust prime minister looked over and cracked a nervous smile as he irritably pushed his way past the pilot. The tiny two-seater was not Churchill's cup of tea. As he positioned himself to exit, his coattails inadvertently slapped the pilot's face. The pilot rolled his eyes as Winston grunted, grabbed the aluminum sash, and then pushed outward, making a short leap to the ground.

He straightened out his wrinkled jacket, then purposefully plodded toward the president's car. In his thick British accent he bellowed, "Franklin ol' boy! How grand to get here in one piece." He grabbed the passenger door handle, then peered back at the Piper Cub with an evil eye. "But that bloody little bird nearly killed me! What a perfectly sinful landing."

Franklin chuckled. "Well, PM, these little Piper Cubs don't handle the turbulence too well, especially around here, near the gusty Hudson. Nor is this one of America's greatest airfields." Franklin adjusted the round spectacles on his nose and added, "However, I'm glad you made it safe and sound. Hop in!"

Churchill swung open the door, placed one foot on the running board, and pulled himself up. Then swiveling his hips, he plopped his rear onto the thick leather seat. Just then, Winston's eyes jolted as they caught a glimpse of the customized control levers. Immediately, they darted back up at Franklin.

Roosevelt winked. "Don't worry! You're in good hands."

"Y…y…yes, ol' chap, I can see. Good hands indeed! But how in blazes can this thing move without foot pedals?"

Franklin laughed. "Right here, with these levers. I have complete control of the throttle and brakes. I can make this baby purr like a cat or scream like a cheetah."

The president squeezed the accelerator lever and the Ford lunged forward, snapping Winston's head clean back. With a startled look, the prime minister forced his head forward, and balked, "Damn cowboys, you Yanks!"

Franklin popped his long, silver cigarette holder into his mouth, and jumped right into positing serious strategies for the war. Winston anxiously righted himself in the seat and tried to listen as Franklin raced along the Hudson's perilous cliffs at nail-biting speed.

With more than a touch of concern, Winston squeaked, "Franklin, ol' boy, I do hope these bloody contraptions of yours have been well tested?"

"Nope! Just had them installed yesterday—I guess you can call this a test drive!"

Winston's eyeballs bulged as he swallowed a lump of fear. Franklin looked over with his trademark grin. As he began to speak, his cigarette holder flapped wildly with each syllable. "Only kidding, Winston. Why sure, these babies are made of the finest U.S. steel. Naturally they were tested. Relax!"

With trepidation, Winston managed to summon enough courage to force a meager smile of confidence. Wearily, Winston proceeded to respond to the critical war strategies and the dilemmas that plagued them both. The further they engaged in conversation, the more Winston forgot about the risky road hazards. All distractions vanished, however, when Franklin unexpectedly mentioned his thoughts about a major strike that would be either a military milestone or a calamitous nightmare.

A profound look of doubt marred Churchill's meaty face. "Franklin, the British military has thoroughly examined the possibilities of a major strike on the northern shores of France, but alas, it came to no avail, and for good reason. Unless by some miracle the German forces become demoralized, I can't fathom how anything of the sort shall ever succeed."

"Winston, we must move boldly and decisively to penetrate Germany with an aggressive assault. We just need to firm up a plan by logically weighing all the options and possible reprisals, so we can knock this bastard on his ass!"

Winston snorted. "Franklin, ol' boy, Britain has been fending for survival for quite some time now, and with all due respect, we're acutely acquainted with German forces. And dare I say, in total confidence, Mr. President, that the German war machine is an intrepid foe, with first-rate generals and superior armaments."

Unflinchingly, Franklin maintained his aggressive stance, as he blazed over the tree-lined country roads. Driving up the pebbled driveway of the Roosevelt estate, which picturesquely overlooked the Hudson River, Franklin and Winston were greeted by Harry Hopkins.

Hopkins was Franklin's personal envoy who was sent to London several years prior to secretly assess Churchill. It was Hopkins who relayed to Roosevelt that, despite popular rumor, especially put forth by Joseph Kennedy, Churchill was not a rhetorical drunkard, but in fact, was the firm and lucid spirit of England itself.

As usual, Hopkins had been waiting with a wheelchair by the main entrance. Franklin swung open the door and slithered his body into the chair. Grabbing the chair's two big front wheels, Franklin pushed himself forward with an affable smile and entered the house.

Winston looked at Harry and raised his eyebrows as they mindfully followed. Up ahead, they saw Franklin eagerly wheel himself over to a glass showcase, then pivot around. As they approached, Franklin enthusiastically showed Winston his prized stamp collection. Winston nodded amicably and listened. At one point he discreetly peered over at Hopkins and winked. After an informative presentation by the president, Winston seized the soapbox to expound upon *his* love for oil painting, which he said began at age forty-one in 1915. However, he regretted not having touched a brush since 1940, as the war had consumed his every waking hour. After which, they all entered the Green Room and enjoyed a cordial dinner with Eleanor and several of her lady friends.

After dessert, Franklin retreated to his study as his two guests followed close behind. As they entered the dimly lit room, Franklin quickly swiveled about in his wheelchair. "Winston, Harry, can I get you boys a drink?"

Winston chuckled. "When did I ever refuse, my dear boy?" he replied, as Harry laughed and nodded.

"Would you boys like the usual, or do you feel adventurous?" As both stood momentarily mute with indecision, Franklin added, "Fine then, how about one of my Orange Blossom Specials?"

Winston waved his hand. "No thank you! I'll stick to my Scotch, ol' boy. Those bloody cocktails of yours are vile concoctions."

Harry laughed and added, "Sure, I'll go for one of your Orange Blossoms, Chief."

Collecting their drinks, the three men clinked rims and toasted.

"Cheers!"

"Salute!"

"Good luck!"

As Winston and Harry took their seats, the prime minister squirmed in his chair as he extracted one of his thickly rolled cigars from his pocket. Striking a match, he lit up the brown, pungent stick.

The president paused as his genial face suddenly grew serene and formal. "Winston, I have something extremely important that I wish to share with you."

With a serious look and a squinted eye, Winston replied, "Franklin, you know you speak as if to your own soul, ol' boy. Go on."

Franklin took a big swig and slowly leaned forward. "Back in October of 1939, an advisor of mine, Alexander Sachs, handed me a letter from the famed Nobel Prize winner, Albert Einstein; whom you've met in the past. This man of great intelligence had made clear to me that a revolutionary new bomb could be fabricated. It's called an atomic bomb. This volatile weapon, he claims, would be of such a magnitude as to lay waste to an entire city."

Winston pulled the smoldering cigar away from his moistened lips and smiled. "Yes, I was already briefed by one of my advisors about this same devilish device, Franklin. I believe it was two months previous, in August of the same year. Odd indeed, how these top secrets are *not* so secret. Aye? In fact, we've already started tinkering with this wild theory, we call it *Tube Alloys*."

"Do you really believe there's much validity to this theory?"

Winston frowned as his deep gravelly voice belched, "May God forgive us; but, yes, I believe so. We inherited two

Jewish scientists from Germany—Otto Robert Frisch and Rudolf Peierls—and they've already laid some groundwork for developing this fiendish monstrosity."

Franklin squinted and paused for a brief moment, then said, "Well, I think it's best if we pool our resources."

"Indeed, man, indeed we must! This new bomb could prove to be a decisive advantage, or foretell the inevitable doom of opening Pandora's Box."

"Well, Winston, as you must know, this apparently ill-kept secret is also known by the Germans. So this is now a race, and not something I can ponder idly anymore. I had allocated only limited resources to this project back in 1939, but now, well, after your confirmation of its true feasibility, I swear by the good Lord above that I have every intention of winning this race. This project will be a top priority and I'll spare no expense." Franklin's face grew stiff with resolve as he added, "We *will* win this race, Winston, and the war!"

Winston shook his head with a dubious grin. "You damn Yanks are a curious lot. Using only mere logic you set a plan into motion, and then inexorably forge forward. A rather grand mindset, if I do say."

Franklin grabbed the bottle of Beefeaters and added another splash of gin to his cocktail. "Yes, Winston, perhaps it is, but defensive maneuvers will not bring about victory. We believe in establishing aggressive goals and achieving them at all costs."

Winston looked at Franklin with paternal gravity beyond his years as he took another puff. As his cigar's peppery smoke rose into his eyes, Winston blinked, and opined, "Franklin, ol' boy, we Britons are most comfortable with improvisation. The battlefield is like a raging sea; you never know when a gale will snap a mast, or a wave will roll a ship. I guess you can say, we Brits roll with the punches."

"Well, PM, we Americans like to throw the punches!"

Churchill laughed with a piggish snort as smoke streamed out his nostrils. "Yes, I can see, ol' boy, I can bloody well see!"

The two leaders spent the next few days soaking up the tranquil scenery of the Hudson Valley. Franklin took Winston on a small tour of the area, pointing out one of Vanderbilt's mansions down the road, and further north the Olana House, designed and once owned by the famous nineteenth century painter, Frederic Church. The eclectic Middle Eastern designs of the small castle intrigued Winston, and since it had been turned into a museum, Churchill couldn't resist taking a guided tour. Only small samples of Church's famous landscapes were on view, but Winston reveled in the art and relaxing conversation. Continuing their leisurely drive, the rural beauties of mountains, dense woods, and the mighty Hudson River offered the two weary leaders much-needed respite. However, by dawn on Sunday, it was time for them and Hopkins to catch a train to Washington, D.C.

The balmy June air peacefully blanketed the mountains, yet as they traveled south they could see dark clouds beginning to form on the horizon. Upon their arrival, the sky rumbled and moaned. As they made their way toward the White House, gusts of wind swirled and drizzle speckled the pavement. En route to the entrance, a torrential downpour unleashed itself upon the trio. Instantly, they were all saturated, as Franklin's hands had all to do to propel the slippery wheels on his chair. Just as they made it over the threshold, the skies cracked, releasing an even heavier deluge of rain that pounded the six-paneled door and windowpanes.

Entirely drenched, Franklin gazed up at Churchill with his typical jovial smile and buoyant inner spirit. "That was rather fun! Are you okay, PM?"

"Certainly, ol' boy. We brawny Brits were reared in the rain. We ought to have gills."

Franklin laughed as he thought about his younger days in the Navy. He had weathered all sorts of storms and swam like a fish. How he missed those years. But the nation had become his salvation, keeping his mind and crippled body active as he diligently struggled to resuscitate it from the ravages of the Great Depression and now from the ultimate peril of conquest by Hitler and Hirohito's war machines. He gazed up at Hopkins, his arms tired from all the wheeling about. "Well, Harry, what do you say you give the old man a push?"

Hopkins dutifully nodded and wheeled Franklin down the hall, as two strips of water and a set of footprints trailed behind. Churchill snapped his saturated derby and followed, as his shoes oozed water from their seams.

However, the rain and the elements were the least of Franklin's worries as they made their way down the slippery hallway. Upon entering the Oval Office, several aides readily stood by, each anxious to update the president. One bent over and whispered into the president's ear.

Twisting in his wheelchair, he looked back at Winston and said, "PM, make yourself comfortable. I'll only be a moment."

The prime minister amicably nodded, then strolled over to the office's huge double-hung windows. As Winston gazed up to ponder the unstable skies, a violent discharge of lightning bolted toward the ground. His plump ruddy face was suddenly illuminated as an aide slowly approached him. The prime minister turned and was cordially presented with his usual Scotch and a coaster bearing the presidential seal.

With a gracious nod, Churchill mindfully turned back to view the tempestuous activity outside. The menacing clouds mercilessly choked the entire sky, while bolts of lightning flashed down from the heavens, as if thunderbolts hurled by enraged pagan gods to punish and decimate humanity. He couldn't help but notice how it unnervingly echoed the war-ridden world they had now found themselves embroiled in.

Meanwhile, another aide quickly entered the office and approached Franklin with a grave look on his face. He handed the president a telegram.

Unfolding the document, Franklin's eyes oscillated left to right and steadily downward. Suddenly his arm fell limp as he turned toward Winston. "PM, I've just received a telegraph. It's regarding your troops in Tobruk."

Winston pivoted about excitedly, when another alarming bolt of lightning flashed. Illuminating Churchill from behind, it formed a brief but ominous silhouette. As Winston spotted Franklin's solemn expression, however, a porcelain-like pallor washed over his face.

With profound misgivings, Winston uttered, "I was expecting good news, but I surmise I'll need another shot before reading this one, aye?"

Franklin sat speechless, his empathetic eyebrows wilted. With a sigh, the president nodded as his line of vision fell solemnly toward the floor.

Winston suddenly felt alone. There he stood, in a foreign office with foreign dignitaries all locked in a cold stare. A wave of discomfort rattled his body. Raising his glass, he threw back his head and emptied his charge in one swig. As the intoxicating tonic slid down his gullet, Winston closed his eyes. Then as he lowered his head, they reopened, a liquored glaze coating each orb. Firmly, he grasped the bottom of his jacket and tugged it down. Taking a deep breath, he advanced toward the president.

Franklin handed Winston the telegram, then swiveled about and rolled slowly toward his desk. With the telegram locked tightly in his hand, Churchill could sense the weight of anticipation by all those in the office. With a feeling of dread, Winston lowered his head to examine the ominous slip.

An eerie silence befell the room. Only the sound of pounding rain and occasional clashes of thunder reverberated within the oval chamber. As Winston read further and further, his heart became weaker and weaker. Then his eyes came to the lethal lines. His soul dropped.

Angrily, Winston crumbled the yellow paper in his meaty fist, and stared gloomily at the floor. Barely detecting a chair nearby, Winston wearily swiveled and plopped backward, sinking into the dark brown leather.

For an odd moment, Winston just sat frozen and mute. Then in his thick British accent, he mumbled as if in a trance, "How could they? I'm utterly appalled. Over 30,000 men surrendered in Tobruk. Only a short while ago, 85,000 surrendered at Singapore. What are these bloody fools thinking? How could they disgrace the Crown like this? Don't they realize civilization and freedom teeter in the balance?" His voice grew heavier, deeper. "Surrender is *not* an option. Damn them! Damn them all!"

His dazed eyes drifted toward Roosevelt. "Dear God, I can just picture Rommel's face. Soon the desert rogue will have access to Cairo and the Suez. This is grave, grave indeed, I tell you. If Hitler allies with Japan, who will move in from the east, they'll occupy the entire breadth of Africa and lower Asia. The oil-rich nations will be theirs. All will be lost!"

Franklin wheeled himself near Winston's side, and placed his hand firmly on his shoulder. Overwhelmed with empathy, he said, "What can we do to help?"

As if awoken from a hellish dream, Winston's glazed eyes cleared. "Franklin, your magnanimity never ceases to amaze. Here I sit dejected, nay, aghast, ashamed, and awaiting a barrage of criticism, yet you rally to my side like a heavenly angel."

Looking about, Winston could see and feel the same spirit and benevolence in the eyes of Franklin's aides. With renewed vigor, Winston energetically rose to his feet. "Give us as many Sherman tanks as you can spare, and ship them to Northern Africa as quickly as possible!"

Without delay, Franklin wheeled himself over to his desk and picked up the phone. Jamming his fingers into the rotary dial, he made direct contact with General George Marshall and duly put in the request.

On the other end, Marshall promptly responded, "But Mr. President, the new Shermans were allotted to one of our own divisions. They're eager to replace their obsolete armaments." Yet, sensing the urgency of the president's request, Marshall switched gears and added, "But, if the British are in dire straits, Mr. President, then the Shermans they will have. I can also send them some newly developed automatic weapons that will prove most useful. Where do we ship them, sir?"

As Roosevelt issued General Marshall the instructions, he looked over at Winston. Giving a firm nod, the president winked. With a profound sense of relief, Winston gazed blissfully at Franklin, awash with veneration.

†††

This vignette recreates an intense moment in time when two great leaders were forced to keep some sense of normalcy while confronting huge obstacles and making critical decisions. It featured the factual events of Winston's visit to America and the wartime decisions and dilemmas of both great leaders. FDR would begin the Manhattan Project in earnest, despite it being a huge gamble of time, money, and valuable resources.

Meanwhile, FDR's supply of Sherman tanks and artillery to Northern Africa played a decisive role in the British victory at El Alamein. The Tobruk debacle was only abated by the solid partnership of Franklin and Winston. Their deep and friendly roots were the result of long, grave struggles together that only hardened their resolve. After the devastating shock of Pearl Harbor, Roosevelt could readily empathize with Churchill when *he* was faced with humiliating defeats. This dynamic relationship was the most important in the twentieth century and was paramount to the Western world's very survival.

During the preliminary years, before America officially joined the war, the British were primarily engaged in responsive tactics, striving to hold the Germans at bay. As Great Britain faced several major setbacks, Roosevelt vigorously rallied support for his friend personally, by lifting his spirits, and physically, by supplying the British with armaments. Due to Roosevelt's struggles with Congress and an isolationist public, America entered the war late; as such, it was not fully mobilized. Fortunately, Roosevelt was clairvoyant, as well as shrewd, and had anticipated the inevitable, for he already had factories retrofitted and engaged in military production before entering the war. Moreover, FDR established his Lend-Lease program, which supplied Britain and the Allied Forces with crucial supplies.

Meanwhile, Churchill made no illusions about Britain's early role and the world's indebtedness to them for being the sole defenders of civilization. In the days and months ahead, the astounding rise of American ingenuity and facility proved awe-inspiring, not only to Churchill but more so to Josef Stalin. At their famous meeting in Teheran, Stalin stated point blank that the success of the war, at that point, was due to the Americans, since their unrivalled production of military machines surpassed that of Britain and Russia combined. As such, the dynamics of world power were inevitably shifting, to Churchill's chagrin.

As a staunch imperialist, Churchill advocated his king and queen's policy of global colonization. This caused a major rift between Roosevelt and Churchill as the president was already assessing the order of the postwar world. This led to Roosevelt's evasive actions at Teheran that baffled and even offended his sentimental British friend. They may have been close friends, but America's future weighed heavier on Franklin's scale of priorities.

Over the ensuing years, Winston's British empire crumbled while Franklin's United States became the ultimate superpower devoted to democracy and freedom. Yet despite each nation's respective fall and rise, the fight to eliminate Hitler's brutal Third Reich had been victorious. The darkness of Hitler's bloody regime, born in the bowels of Hell and inculcated with hatred, was expunged, as the light of a new dawn shed its rays on a grateful free world. Integrity had conquered hatred.

Thank You

To all the great sources of inspiration, from novelists to nonfiction and from all the other sources of media that have fed my imagination, I thank you!

To my steadfast family and friends who have supported my creative endeavors and my editors, marketers and to all the international contest judges who have voted several of my books as award winners, I am most grateful. *Thank you!*

— Rich DiSilvio

THE AUTHOR

Rich DiSilvio is an author of thrillers, mysteries, historical fiction and nonfiction. He has written books, historical articles, and commentaries for magazines and online resources. His passion for history, art, music, and architecture has yielded contributions in each discipline in his professional careers.

DiSilvio's work in the entertainment industry includes projects for historical documentaries, including James Cameron's *The Lost Tomb of Jesus, Killing Hitler, The War Zone* series, *Return to Kirkuk, Operation Valkyrie,* and cable TV shows and films such as *Tracey Ullman's State of the Union, Celebrity Mole, Blood Ties, Monty Python: Almost the Truth,* and many others.

He has written commentaries on the great composers (such as the top-rated Franz Liszt Site), and conceived and designed the Pantheon of Composers porcelain collection for the Metropolitan Opera, which also retailed throughout the USA and Europe.

His artwork and new media projects have graced the album covers and animated advertisements for numerous super-groups and celebrities, including, Pink Floyd, Yes, The Moody Blues, Cher, Madonna, Jay-Z, Willie Nelson, Miles Davis, the Rolling Stones, Alice Cooper, Queen, and many more.

As a software designer/developer, Rich pioneered the first interactive CD-ROM for educating staff and parents about Applied Behavioral Analysis (ABA) for training individuals with autism.

Rich lives in New York with his wife and has four children.

My Nazi Nemesis

GOLD AWARD WINNER

★★★★★ "DiSilvio's plot is cunning and ingenious!"
-- *Jack Magnus for Readers' Favorite*

A deadly love triangle launches a father and daughter team to hunt down a nefarious Nazi. Yet twists and turns abound, leading to a shocking climax.

Hardcover: 9780981762586
Paperback: 9780981762579
eBook: 9780981762593

A Blazing Gilded Age

INTERNATIONAL AWARD WINNER

A riveting rags-to-riches saga about a poor family's struggle to survive amid a nation burning with ambition yet bleeding with injustice. Features, Teddy Roosevelt, JP Morgan, Mark Twain, Tesla and more.

Lauded by HISTORY/A+E and noted biographer Roger DiSilvestro.

Hardcover: 9780981762562
Paperback: 9780981762555
eBook: 9780997680720

Tales of Titans Series

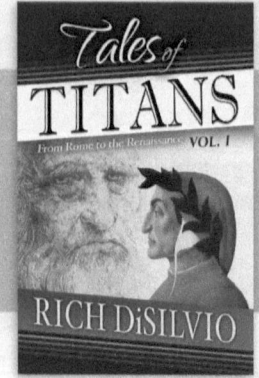 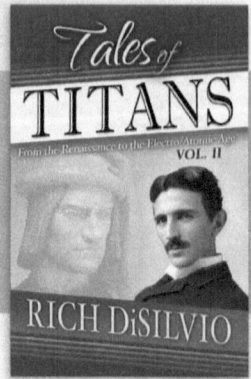 

Tales of Titans brings great historical figures to life with concise yet compelling essays, coupled with engaging narratives that enlighten readers to their miraculous deeds, and misdeeds, that have significantly shaped Western civilization.

This handsomely illustrated series offers readers brief biographical overviews and cogent analysis, while the quasi-fictional scenarios transport readers into a fascinating past, whereby putting flesh on the bones of several titans and offering glimpses into their hearts, minds, and actions.

Tales of Titans, Vol. I : From Rome to the Renaissance
Augustus & Livia, Vespasian & Titus, Hadrian, Constantine, Dante, Brunelleschi, Columbus, Vespucci, King Ferdinand, Pope Alexander VI & Cesare Borgia, and Leonardo da Vinci.

Tales of Titans, Vol. II: Renaissance to the Electro/Atomic Age
The Medicis, Gutenberg, Lorenzo de Medici, Savonarola, Leonardo & Machiavelli, Martin Luther, Queen Elizabeth I, Shakespeare, Galileo, Darwin, Marx, Stalin, Freud, Marconi, Edison, Tesla, Westinghouse, Einstein, Fermi and von Braun.

Tales of Titans, Vol. III: Founding Fathers, Women Warriors & WWII
Samuel Adams, Thomas Paine, George Washington, John Adams, Thomas Jefferson, James Madison, Alexander Hamilton, Ben Franklin, Sybil Ludington, James Armistead Lafayette, Elizabeth Cady Stanton, Susan B. Anthony, Harriet Tubman, Adolf Hitler, FDR & Churchill

Liszt's *Dante Symphony*

A historical mystery/thriller highlighting the belligerent rise of Nazi Germany from its Prussian roots, replete with ciphers, spies, murder and a stellar cast, including Albert Einstein, Rossini, Liszt, Nazi officers and Adolf Hitler.

Hardcover: 9780981762548
Paperback: 9780981762531
eBook: 9780997680713

The Winds of Time

The Winds of Time is a historical tour de force of Western civilization by Rich DiSilvio.

With masterful style, DiSilvio paints a fascinating historical canvas with the flare of a consummate artist. Key figures and the primary cultures that literally shaped the Western world are candidly analyzed, revealing both the dark and luminous sides of mankind. Moreover, DiSilvio's insightful essays add intriguing new dimensions to the historical record.

Hardcover: 9780981762524
eBook: 9780997680706

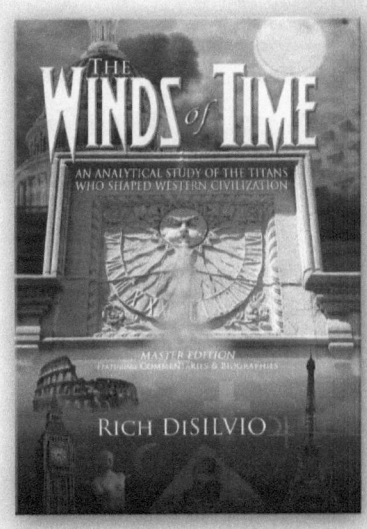

SILVER MEDAL WINNER
Meet My Famous Friends

Inspiring kids with Humor!
A whimsical picture book that pays homage to great historical figures in imaginative ways.

Author/Illustrator Rich DiSilvio presents a broad array of geniuses and heroes in a humorous and compelling fashion by altering their names and appearances, whereby making us see very familiar people in very different ways.

While children will get a kick out of looking at the comical artwork, teens and even adults will appreciate the witty play on words, inventive creations, and perhaps glean a thing or two about some of these iconic people who had a great influence on society in one form or another. Their lives and contributions have uplifted humanity in various ways, thus being great role models for young and old alike.

Hardcover: 9780997680751 Paperback: 9780997680768 eBook: 9780997680775

PURPLE DRAGONFLY WINNER
Danny and the DreamWeaver

A MS novelette by Mark Poe (aka Rich DiSilvio) about the power of dreams and the imagination.

When Danny meets Nostrildamus in his dream a bizarre journey begins!

Packed with dry humor, a mystery, and zany-looking artists, like Michelanjello & Hippopotamus Bosch, *Danny and the DreamWeaver* is an imaginative adventure of criminal intrigue and art history that demonstrates the importance of looking at life differently.

Paperback: 9780997680737
eBook: 9780997680744

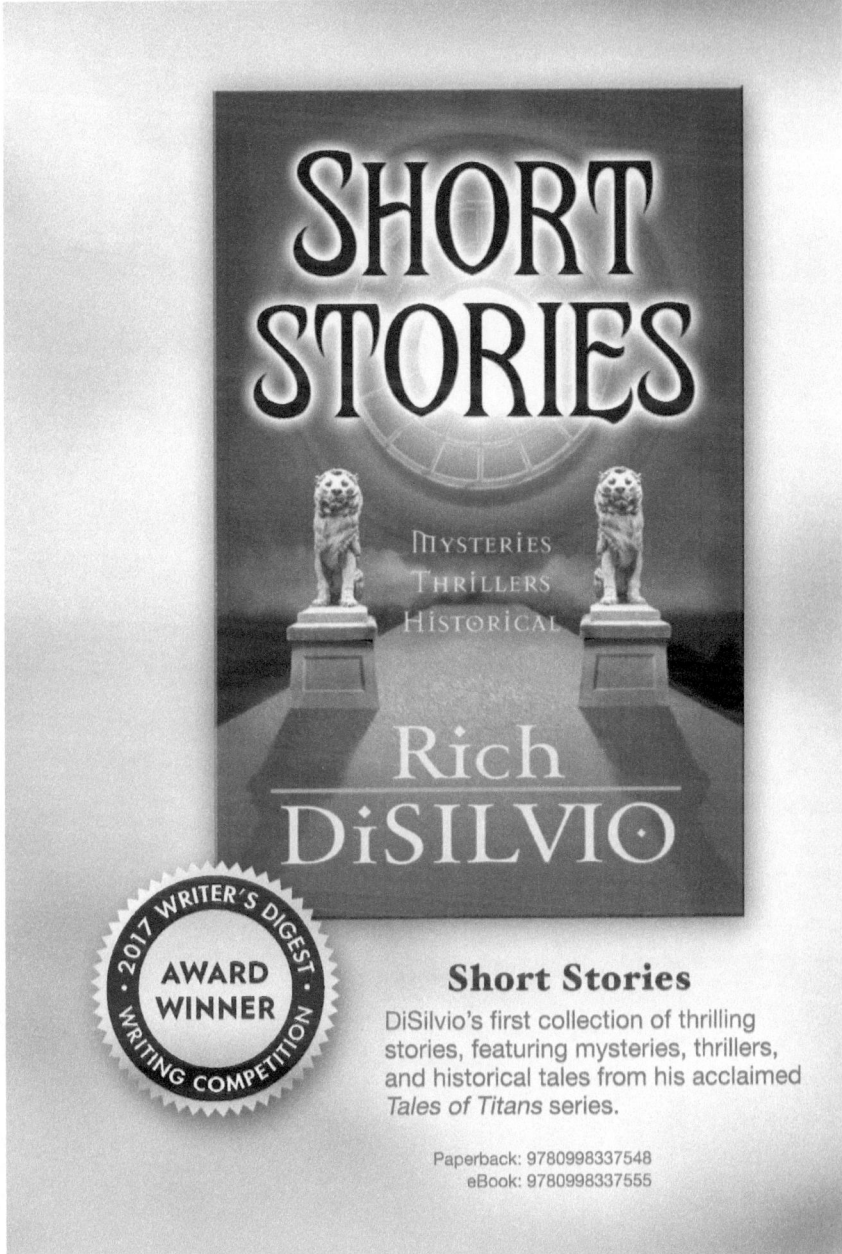

Short Stories

DiSilvio's first collection of thrilling stories, featuring mysteries, thrillers, and historical tales from his acclaimed *Tales of Titans* series.

Paperback: 9780998337548
eBook: 9780998337555